You can be your dream, a voice inside her said.

She closed her hands around the rock, and warm vibrations radiated through her body.

Put it under your pillow and dream your dreams. You can be your dream. You can be your dream.

Marilee slipped the rock under her pillow, lay down, and closed her eyes.

"Sleeping with a rock under my head might mean I have rocks *in* my head," she said out loud, yawning.

Marilee smiled. *I wish I were rich,* she thought. *So rich that I could do whatever I wanted and no one could ever humiliate me again and Adam would love me and not Olivia.*

Mirror Image books
by Cherie Bennett and Jeff Gottesfeld

Stranger in the Mirror
Rich Girl in the Mirror
Star in the Mirror *(coming April 2000)*

Rich Girl in the Mirror

MIRROR IMAGE

Cherie Bennett

and

Jeff Gottesfeld

AN ARCHWAY PAPERBACK
Published by POCKET BOOKS
New York London Toronto Sydney Singapore

This book is a work of fiction. Names, characters, places and incidents are products of the authors' imagination or are used fictitiously. Any resemblance to actual events or locales or persons, living or dead, is entirely coincidental.

AN ARCHWAY PAPERBACK *Original*

 An Archway Paperback published by
POCKET BOOKS, a division of Simon & Schuster Inc.
1230 Avenue of the Americas, New York, NY 10020

ISBN: 0-671-03631-9

First Archway Paperback printing February 2000

10 9 8 7 6 5 4 3 2 1

AN ARCHWAY PAPERBACK and colophon are registered trademarks of Simon & Schuster Inc.

Front cover illustration by Kamil Vojnar

Printed in the U.S.A.

IL 5+

for our readers

Rich Girl in the Mirror

Prologue

** NATIONAL SECURITY MEMORANDUM #1 **
EXTREME TOP SECRET, EYES-ONLY,
LIMITED DISTRIBUTION

THIS IS COPY NUMBER 8 OUT OF 15 TOTAL

From: Dr. Louise Warner, Chair, Substance Z project
To: Substance Z Recovery/Field Test Team
Re: Substance Z Effect on Teenage Girls

All members of the Substance Z (Sub Z) Recovery and Field Test Team (SZR/FTT) are well aware of the partial destruction of a top-secret Substance Z satellite, code-named Subbie, the unplanned return to earth of its activated Sub Z payload, and the bizarre effects of that Sub Z on one American teen girl who contacted a chunk of it.

After Subbie exploded, chunks of active Sub Z scattered across much of southern Louisiana and southeast Texas. Fortunately, the media reported the explosion as an incoming meteor.

Our teams have documented the recovery of a glasslike, beautifully formed chunk of highly active Sub Z, by one Callie Bailey, 15, a New Orleans high school sophomore. Bailey, a self-described geek girl, became absolutely beautiful as a result of her contact with Sub Z. It was a classic Mirror Image Effect (MIE). Bailey was able to reverse the MIE. How? We don't know.

We put Bailey under surveillance and treated her experience as a field test of Sub Z. But the Bailey field test raises as many questions as it answers:

1. Does activated Sub Z affect only teenage females?

2. Does contact with Sub Z affect only the physical characteristics of a person, or can it, in effect, put the person's entire life "through the looking glass" and *turn her into the opposite of what she once was?*

3. How long-lasting is the effect?
4. How does the MIE reverse itself?

Covert ops was able to attach a radio transmitter to Bailey's chunk of Sub Z. But both Bailey's chunk of Sub Z and the transmitter were lost. Therefore, we do not know who, if anyone, now has Bailey's chunk of Sub Z.

Mission orders, then, are as follows:

1. Search out the chunks of Sub Z that reached the ground. *Use extreme caution in handling!*
2. Determine who, if anyone, may now be holding Bailey's chunk of Sub Z, and monitor for the Mirror Image Effect.
3. Assess the national security implications of the above.

There is no need to remind you that our work is being followed by those at the highest levels of the government, NASA, and the Department of Defense, but I will stress this fact anyway. That is all.

DESTROY THIS MEMORANDUM FOLLOWING READING.

Chapter

1

*W*hat would you do, *Adam Eagleton,* Marilee Ellis thought, *if I leaned across this counter right this minute, grabbed you by your T-shirt, and kissed you?*

Marilee's hand instantly flew to her mouth in embarrassment, as if she had blurted out the words instead of only thinking them. Adam had been her best guy friend for two years, and he knew her better than just about anyone in the world. Well, except for Karly Renwick, of course. Karly was more like a sister than a friend, but Karly now lived several towns away from Marilee.

Whatever. What mattered at this very moment was how great it was that Adam could not read her mind.

"Did you say something, Marilee?" Adam asked as he handed a customer a receipt.

"Me? Say something? Nope, uh-uh, nothing," Marilee said quickly. Wow. Wait till she told Karly about this one. If Adam was starting to read her thoughts, she was in big trouble.

Because then he'd know everything.

How her feelings about him had changed practically overnight, from best friend to—well, to thoughts and dreams that made her blush. Even when she talked about them with Karly.

Anyway, it was all Adam's fault.

As soon as school had ended the previous June, Adam's parents had sent him from Overton, the upscale suburb of New Orleans where Marilee and he both lived, to visit some relatives in Maine. He'd left Louisiana his smart, funny, best-friend self. His short and very, very skinny best-friend self.

Maybe it was the Maine water. Because Adam returned to Louisiana ten weeks later this tall, cute hunk. He had muscles. And a dimple in his chin. And he just . . . well, he was the same Adam inside. But outside was an entirely different story.

Marilee wasn't the only one who had noticed his transformation. Last year the rich, popular girls at Overton High would not give Adam the time of day. But now they had all turned into organic food junkies. It gave them a perfect excuse to stop by his parents' health food store, Overton Naturals, whenever he was working.

As if they're actually going to go into their kitchens and whip up a tasty soy loaf, Marilee thought wryly.

Adam seemed to love the idea that the richest girls at Overton High School were flirting with him. Just as he always had, he confided in Marilee about which girl had invited him where, or who had called him on some silly pretext to talk to him.

How could he be flattered by such idiotic girls? It made Marilee really crazy. And really jealous.

"He's just a guy, Marilee," Karly told her when they talked on the phone, which was practically every night. "Before, you were the only girl who paid attention to him and that was different."

"Well, he was different then," Marilee replied.

"Externally," Karly reminded her. "He's the same inside."

"Then why do I feel so stupid around him now?"

" 'Cuz you're getting all hung up on the external Adam," Karly said. "I know. Pretend he's one of the stray animals you take care of."

Marilee laughed at this. She took in stray animals—from dogs to cats to birds to rabbits— and nurtured them back to health. Last year, pre–Adam-the-hunk, the two of them had built a special area for the animals behind the trailer where she and her dad lived.

Then, it was easy for us to be best friends, she thought. *The two poorest kids in Overton. You and me against the world in a brother-and-sister kind of way. But how can I tell him my feelings have gone from strictly platonic to monumentally romantic?*

Answer: I can't.

Adam waited on the next customer as Marilee checked her watch and sighed. The guy at the counter wanted five types of beans in bulk. At this rate Adam wouldn't get a break. Marilee had to be at her after-school waitress job in fifteen minutes. And she really needed to talk to him.

Marilee watched as he lifted a huge sack of pinto beans, his sinewy muscles flexing inside his blue-and-white Overton Naturals T-shirt.

Her mind recorded his image in a mental photograph as vivid as any she'd taken for her basic photography course at Overton High School. She loved that course and photography so much that her heart sang every time she picked up a camera.

She studied Adam now.

The short hair the same shade as the dark grand piano in the Calhouns' mammoth living room. The intense blue eyes the color of the sky just before dusk. The chiseled jawline. The strong arms that could hold her so tenderly.

The soft lips that would laugh hysterically if she told him the truth about her feelings.

Quit it, she ordered herself. *You're driving your-*

self nuts. Maybe after you're a famous National Geographic *photographer and he's a big musician, he'll love you back.*

She could just picture Karly's amused reaction to that concept.

Marilee caught Adam's eye and made a "hurry up" gesture that got a wink from her friend. Adam was now weighing out raw cashews for Mrs. Layton, who looked as if she'd just stepped out of some tennis magazine.

Imagine having a mom who looks like that, Marilee thought. *Of course, if my mom was still alive, I wouldn't care if she was green or bald or looked like a troll, I'd love her more than anyone ever loved her mother.*

Stop daydreaming, Marilee told herself.

The chimes on the front door of the health food store tinkled. Overton High School's reigning snob, Olivia Fairmont, and her best friend, Bree—Mrs. Layton's daughter—burst into the store.

Marilee inwardly rolled her eyes. Olivia and Bree were fifteen, just like she was. Both were filthy rich. Wore the right clothes. Had the right hair and the right makeup. Were really beautiful.

And really, really intimidating.

It didn't matter to Marilee that her father and grandmother and even Karly insisted that she was pretty. Adam had once told her that she looked a lot like a brunette version of the alternative singer-songwriter Jewel, and everyone thought Jewel was so cool and gorgeous.

But that was pre-hunk Adam, so it didn't count.

When Marilee had first moved to Overton from Carter, she felt shy around all the rich kids. She'd tried being nice to everyone she met at school, even Livy and Bree. But the two girls had acted so superior to Marilee—obviously because they thought she was a poor girl who wasn't up to their "standards"—that Marilee had given up speaking to them.

Karly, who'd met them once at the mall, had awarded them first place in the Two Most Superficial Girls on the Planet contest. A contest that, of course, Karly had invented.

Why is it, Marilee thought sadly, *that animals respond with love when you give them love, but some people are hateful to you no matter what you do? I bet if I was rich like they are, they'd treat me like a human being.*

"Oh, hi, Livy," Mrs. Layton said to the girls. "Bree, darling, did you drop Oodles off at the groomer?"

Bree nodded. Her mother bent to kiss her cheek, but Bree feinted away.

"I'm just going to take a quick run through the veggies," Mrs. Layton told Bree, ignoring her gesture.

"Take your time. I'll get a ride home with Livy," Bree said. "We ran into each other at Zazu."

Livy lifted a glossy black shopping bag with a shocking pink logo that read ZAZU. Zazu was one of the high-priced boutiques in Overton Square. The least expensive thing there cost more than Marilee earned in a month. Marilee had been inside once. She remembered the salesgirl named Roxie who had looked at her jeans disdainfully and suggested that Marilee ought to leave. Immediately.

Mrs. Layton hurried to the vegetable section as Olivia and Bree casually ambled over to Adam's counter.

As if Adam isn't the real reason they're here, Marilee thought. *These girls wouldn't know organic food if it jumped up and bit them on the butt!*

"Hi, Adam," Olivia said with a flirtatious smile. Neither she nor Bree acknowledged Marilee's presence.

"How's it going?" Bree added.

"Fine," Adam replied easily. "What's up?"

Olivia launched into some breezy story about how she and her friends were going riding together that weekend.

Marilee coughed ostentatiously to get Adam's attention.

"Hey, excuse me," Adam told the girls with a grin that showed his dimples. "Marilee's been waiting to talk to me and I had all these customers."

"Oh! Hi, Marilee," Bree said, pretending to notice Marilee just then. "Look, we're gonna go check out the new essential oils. We'll be right back, Adam. Okay?"

After the girls had walked away, Marilee trilled, "Oh, Adam, you're just so *cute* standin' there with all those organic thingies."

Her imitation of Olivia was dead-on perfect, and Adam cracked up.

"Buy seven or eight," Marilee called to Livy softly, so the girls couldn't hear but Adam could. "Help the store out. Buy twenty thousand!"

He laughed again. Great dimples.

"You know, when it comes to money, Adam, you have a very bizarre mentality." Marilee glanced at Olivia and Bree again. "I will never understand how your parents could quit jobs in New Orleans to open a health food store in Overton. Good-bye, big house. Good-bye, BMW. Hello, struggling store with dinky apartment over it. *On purpose.*"

"I've told you a million times, Marilee, they hated who they'd become in New Orleans. They're happier now without all that stuff. So am I."

"Well, poor by choice is—no offense, big guy—insane."

"It's all in how you look at it," Adam said

philosophically. "So, what was it you wanted to talk to me about so badly?"

"It's about the—"

"I can't believe it's after four already." An elderly woman pushed past Marilee toward Adam. "Where has the day gone?"

After four?

Marilee looked at her watch. "Mr. Wilson is going to kill me if I'm late again," she groaned, heading for the door. "I'll call you later."

Abruptly she stopped and turned to face him. He raised his eyebrows.

"Sniff mah wrists, Adam, I just put the *cutest* organic oils on!" Marilee purred in her best Olivia voice.

"Get outta here," Adam said, laughing.

Marilee ran the two blocks to Hava Java, the oh-so-hip coffeehouse where she worked. Mr. Wilson, the owner, glared at her as she hurried in the door.

"I know, I know, I'm sorry I'm late, I couldn't help it, I was abducted by aliens," Marilee said breathlessly as she dumped her backpack behind the counter and tied a Hava Java apron over her clothes.

"You were late last week because you were abducted by aliens," he reminded her dryly.

"Amazing, huh?" Marilee smiled at him. "I'll just go . . . waitress. What a good idea."

Hava Java was full and there was only one

other waitress working, so Marilee got very busy very fast. Her job was crucial. The tips she got sometimes made the difference between being able to pay an important bill or not. Marilee's father, the handyman at the Calhoun estate, was terrible with money. Marilee was the one who always had to check that things got paid on time.

"Three almond croissants, one triple-fruit salad, one cappuccino, one hazelnut decaf, two double lattes," Marilee said as she set the orders down in front of four middle-aged women at table 6.

Out of the corner of her eye, Marilee saw Olivia and Bree come into the coffeehouse and plop themselves down at the table for two near the cappuccino machine. The two of them had done more shopping since Marilee had seen them, because they had tons of shopping bags now.

"Well, that was a workout," Bree exclaimed loud enough for Marilee to hear.

Olivia laughed. "Maxed out the credit card again."

Marilee crossed right by their table and said, "I'll be right back to get your order."

If they heard her, they didn't bother to let her know.

"I mean it, Livy, no way am I wearing the formal Gayle wants me to get," Marilee heard Bree say, referring to her mom by her first name. "She wants me in pastels. Pink—"

"Silvery pink," Olivia teased. "Not rose pink."

Bree groaned. "Pastels make me gag. So do mothers."

"We can go into New Orleans and—"

Marilee turned the cappuccino machine on, as much to drown out the girls' inane conversation as to do her job. The girls were talking about Overton High's upcoming fall formal dance. Unlike the prom, which was reserved for juniors and seniors, the fall formal was for the entire high school.

It would be Marilee's first formal dance, ever.

If she was going.

Which did not seem very likely.

For one thing, she didn't have anything to wear. And short of a fairy godmother granting her a magic wish, she wasn't likely to get a formal dress anytime soon.

For another thing, no one had asked her.

Well, that wasn't totally true. Karly had offered to come to Overton and go to Marilee's formal with her. Sometimes girls who didn't have boyfriends went together, so it wouldn't be weird. But as much as Marilee loved Karly, she just didn't want to remember her very first formal as the one she went to with a girlfriend. Not even a best girlfriend.

What she wanted was to go with Adam.

"Here's a crazy idea—ask him," Karly had said as if it were the simplest thing in the world.

Well, maybe that would be simple for Karly. She wasn't afraid of anything or anyone. But Marilee just couldn't do it. The words just would not come out of her mouth.

Sigh. Adam hadn't asked her, either. Not yet, anyway.

"Excuse me, waitress? Marilee?" Bree called to her. "Would you mind taking our order? We're famished."

"As soon as I can," Marilee told them, as she'd told impatient customers a thousand times before.

Suddenly she had the most powerful desire— she wanted her life to change completely. Now.

I wish I could be rich, Marilee thought. *Richer than Olivia and Bree put together. I'd be richer but I'd still be nice. Then Adam would look at me like he looks at Olivia. And he'd pick me over her.*

"Marilee, in this lifetime?" Bree asked impatiently.

And while I'm making wishes, Marilee added in her mind, *let Adam invite me to the fall formal. And let the world's most gorgeous formal dress suddenly appear in my bedroom. In my size. Light blue would be nice.*

Oh, yeah. And matching shoes and bag.

And while I'm at it, how about four new cameras, a lifetime supply of film, and my own darkroom?

And a job at National Geographic *after college?*

And loving homes for all the stray cats in America?

"Marilee!" Bree cawed, really annoyed.

"Coming," Marilee assured her. She smiled faintly at her own ridiculous thoughts and hurried to take Bree's order.

Okay, so her dreams weren't ever going to come true. One great thing about dreams was, the price was right. And dreams were something she could always have more of than Livy or Bree.

Chapter

2

"So, Marilee," Ms. Pfeffer said briskly, "let's open that portfolio and see what you've got."

Marilee's stomach did a flip-flop. Ms. Pfeffer's photography class was by far Marilee's favorite thing about Overton High School. The well-funded school had its own darkroom and equipment, including a wonderful Nikon camera that any student could check out and use, and a budget for film.

More important than even that, Ms. Pfeffer was a wonderful, inspirational teacher. She'd taken a big pay cut when she left a job as a photographer at the *Times-Picayune* newspaper to come teach. Marilee didn't know what had motivated Ms. Pfeffer to do it. Whatever the reason, Marilee was glad that she had.

Most of the time.

At the moment, though, all Marilee felt about Ms. Pfeffer was scared. Ms. Pfeffer was about to assess Marilee's photos in their first private pupil-teacher conference.

Last year, on a total whim, Marilee had chosen an introduction to photography class. It turned out that photography taught her to see the world differently. She found herself studying light and shadow and learning how a facial expression or the juxtaposition of objects could tell a whole story in a single image.

Her favorite thing to photograph was animals, which led to her dream of someday working for *National Geographic*.

This year Marilee was taking basic photography. Anyone could get into basic. But next year, Ms. Pfeffer would have to invite her into advanced photography.

She only accepted a handful of students.

Marilee wanted to be invited almost as much as she wished Adam would look at her the way he now looked at Olivia Fairmont.

"I'm nervous," Marilee confessed to the teacher.

Ms. Pfeffer smiled and pushed some of her short brown hair back behind her ears. "I was just as nervous at my first photo conference."

"Really?"

"Absolutely. It was in college. We were supposed to pick our best ten prints and go over them with our professor."

"I suppose your teacher loved yours," Marilee guessed.

Ms. Pfeffer laughed, her blue eyes bright behind round, wire-rimmed glasses. "Not exactly. You see, I got so crazed trying to choose which ones to show him that I finally decided they were all terrible, that I had no talent, and that I was doomed to failure."

"So what happened?"

"I showed up with an empty portfolio."

Marilee was amazed. "That really happened?"

"It really did. And bless my professor, he was kind enough to let me reschedule. So whatever you show me is better than what I brought in to show him."

Marilee smiled—Ms. Pfeffer's story did make her feel better. She pushed the portfolio across the desk.

Ms. Pfeffer opened it and carefully studied each of the ten photos that Marilee had selected. Marilee sneaked a look at Ms. Pfeffer's face to try to gauge her reaction, but Ms. Pfeffer was unreadable.

After Ms. Pfeffer had gone through all ten photos, she turned back to the first one and studied it as if she were seeing it for the first time.

Marilee had presented three groups of three related pictures, and then a single photo. The first group featured her grandmother, whom Marilee called Grammy, outside Grammy's modest home in Carter, about fifteen miles from Overton. Both the house and the woman in the photo were obviously old and weathered, yet dignified.

At least that was what Marilee hoped.

The second group had been taken at the New Orleans zoo in the big cat area just before feeding time. The look of hunger on the various animals' faces was powerful, and the sense, to Marilee at least, was that the tigers felt in charge of the camera and the person behind it.

The third group of three, also of animals, had been taken behind the trailer. It featured a dog and a mother cat, with her three kittens. In the first photo, the five animals were regarding one another warily. By the third photo, the cats were sleeping curled up at the dog's belly.

The final picture was of Adam on a bare stage, his face half in light, half in shadow, playing his guitar.

Ms. Pfeffer looked at them all again and then looked up at Marilee.

"So," she asked finally, "which is best?"

Marilee shifted uncomfortably in her chair. "I thought you were going to tell me that."

"You first."

"Well," Marilee ventured, "out of all of them, I like the animals in my backyard the most."

Ms. Pfeffer nodded.

"I, uh . . . think the composition is pretty good," Marilee ventured.

" 'Pretty good'?" Ms. Pfeffer raised her eyebrows.

"Okay, the composition is solid," Marilee affirmed. "I guess . . . they tell a story about . . . how things can change."

Bam! Ms. Pfeffer's hand came down hard on the table, and Marilee jumped.

"Exactly!" the teacher exclaimed. "It's a metaphor. These animals are just like us. Think of how we segregate ourselves just because of how we look or dress, or how rich we are or aren't. But when we get to know each other as individuals, everything can change. It's all right there. Three pictures, telling a whole story, not just about these animals, but about all of us."

Hope filled Marilee like helium fills a balloon. She'd felt all those things, but hadn't any idea how to articulate them.

"This is wonderful work, Marilee."

Marilee was thrilled. "Really?"

"Really." Ms. Pfeffer clasped her hands and leaned eagerly toward her pupil. "Have you considered Y.A.A.?"

Only every single waking moment since I heard about it, Marilee thought.

Y.A.A. was the Young Artists Alliance competition, a national arts contest sponsored by a not-for-profit organization based in New York. There was one division for painting, one for sculpture, and one for photography. Three high school student winners were picked in each category, and those nine got to spend the summer at the Rhode Island School of Design, working with some of the most famous art instructors in the world.

Each year Y.A.A. chose a different theme. This year's theme was multimedia. Which meant that an entry could not simply be a painting, or a sculpture, or a photograph. It had to involve more than one art form. For photography, Marilee knew her entry would need something else.

Like, say, music. Original music. Which could be written by her best friend Adam, who wrote some of the most beautiful songs Marilee had ever heard.

That is, if she ever got a chance to ask him.

That was what she'd wanted to ask him at Overton Naturals the day before. She *still* had not had a chance to ask him.

"I've thought about it," Marilee confessed. "But—"

"Cut the negativity," her teacher interrupted. "Your mission is to do your best work. Period. You have no control over anything else. So, what did you have in mind?"

"I was thinking of having slide projections of some of my photos set to an original musical composition."

"Theme?" Ms. Pfeffer asked.

"I don't really know yet," Marilee admitted.

"Music?"

"I don't know that, either, exactly. But my friend Adam—the guitar player in the photo—would write it."

Ms. Pfeffer nodded. "You'll need to figure out specifics, Marilee. The deadline is a month from today."

"I know," Marilee began, "but—"

"But nothing," Ms. Pfeffer cut her off. "Don't set up obstacles for yourself, Marilee. The world is happy to set them up for you. Look, I'll help you any way I can, within the boundaries of the rules."

The teacher closed Marilee's portfolio and pushed it over to her. "Think about the story you were able to tell with the animal photos in your backyard. There may be something in that. And get this friend Adam to work on the perfect original song."

"I'll try," Marilee said softly.

Ms. Pfeffer patted Marilee's hand. "You've got to believe in yourself, Marilee. And believe me— I know from experience that's easier said than done."

Chapter

3

"Grammy?" Marilee called as she opened the door to the trailer where she and her dad lived. She'd seen her grandmother's Ford pickup truck parked off the dirt road that led to the trailer. The trailer itself was at the far reaches of the enormous Calhoun estate.

Grammy lived in Carter. Marilee and her dad used to live there, too. Fifteen miles away, working-class Carter was a place so different from wealthy Overton as to be another planet. But that had never mattered to Marilee, or to Karly, who still lived there. Marilee only wished she still lived there, too. She loved Carter.

Many of the adults in Carter had worked at the auto parts factory. But a few years ago, the owner closed it and moved it to Mexico. More than a hundred people were put out of work, including Marilee's dad.

There were few decent jobs in Carter. So, months later, Marilee's dad accepted a job as the Calhouns' handyman, and he and Marilee had moved to Overton and into the mobile home that Mrs. Calhoun provided them.

In some ways, Overton was an improvement. The schools were better. Marilee had made some new friends. And, of course, there were the photography courses. But Marilee still missed the town she considered home. She couldn't help it. Carter was in her heart. She hated living so far from Grammy.

And especially so far from Karly.

It was not easy being the poorest girl in Overton, where so many people judged you because you lived in a mobile home. True, there wasn't much room in the kitchen because Marilee's dad had turned much of it into a workshop. But the rest of the trailer was reasonably spacious. There was a big living room with a new couch, chair, and a cable-equipped TV. Marilee and her dad each had a bedroom. And the two of them shared a small bathroom, which Karly had dubbed the "bathroomette."

And that was it.

Except for the Big Room, Marilee mentally added. *Can't forget the Big Room.*

The Big Room was what her father jokingly called the lawn outside the trailer where he'd spread out plastic lawn furniture. And where Marilee kept her impromptu menagerie of stray animals.

"We got the biggest and nicest room in Overton," he'd tell Marilee, mussing her hair affectionately. "Those snobs don't got nothin' on us, honey!"

"Grammy?" Marilee called again, dropping her backpack on the couch.

No answer. Huh. Where could Grammy be?

Then, a familiar face wearing a huge grin peeked around the corner from the narrow hallway.

"Karly!" Marilee whooped happily as her friend rushed toward her to give her a hug. Grammy had been hiding right behind Karly, and now watched happily as the two girls laughed and hugged some more.

"You're such a sweetheart, Grammy." Marilee left Karly to hug her grandmother, who was already bustling around the small kitchen.

"So are you," Grammy told Marilee with a smile.

Usually, Marilee and Karly could only see each other on weekends. So it was a major treat for Grammy to have surprised Marilee by bringing Karly to visit on a weekday.

Karly plopped down on the couch. "So, tell me all the latest news about everything." She

blew her shaggy bangs off her forehead, something she did a lot. Karly looked like a teen version of a Raggedy Ann doll, with flaming red hair
and blue eyes. Just looking at her made Marilee
smile.

Marilee sat with her. "Ready to move in with
us? We'll pitch a tent for you outside. That is, if
you're willing to sleep with the strays."

"Not tempting," Karly said. "But I am such a
terrific friend that I fed and watered your brood
for you. You'll get my bill in the mail."

"Lemonade, girls," Grammy called as she
poured them each a glass. "And my famous
peanut butter cookies."

Marilee and Karly dove into the treats.

"I could eat about four dozen of these," Karly
said though a mouthful of cookie.

"Hey, a future firefighter has to keep up her
strength," Marilee teased.

Karly's dad was chief of Carter's fire department. And Karly had announced to Marilee at
age eight that she planned to be a firefighter, too.

"Do you realize that I'll be the first female firefighter in Carter?" Karly asked.

"You can do whatever you set your mind to,
Karly," Grammy said. "You too, Marilee."

"I know that, Grammy," Marilee said softly.
And she did. Most of the time.

"I wish my son knew it," Grammy said with a
sigh. "Gramps and I raised him up to believe in

himself, Marilee. But he hasn't been the same since—well, you know, sweetie."

Marilee nodded.

Grammy smoothed Marilee's hair. "Now, go visit with Karly. We've got to go soon. I left a roast in the oven."

Karly grabbed a handful of cookies and they went to Marilee's room. Marilee knew just what her grandmother had wanted to say when she'd stopped herself; that her father hadn't been the same since Marilee's mother had died all those years ago.

Grammy often recounted how, after he'd graduated from high school, Marilee's father worked in the factory for six weeks. He hated it so much that he took off and hitchhiked to California, where he met and married Marilee's mother. And where Marilee had been born.

Marilee didn't remember California. She didn't remember her mother, either. She had only one photo of her, which she kept, framed, by her bed. According to her father, her mother had been perfect—beautiful inside and out, an angel on earth.

And, according to him, Marilee looked just like her.

"Right down to that heart-shaped beauty mark on your arm," her father would always say. Marilee glanced at her mother's photo now. She couldn't see any resemblance.

Karly took her customary flying leap onto Marilee's bed, landing with a thud. "Grammy is the best," she said, biting into another cookie. "Her showing up got me out of having to cut the grass."

"Can't you get Pete to cut it for you?"

Karly looked up, puzzled. "Pete? Who's Pete? Do you know a *Pete?* Cuz I don't."

Both girls dissolved into peals of laughter. Karly always said the same thing when she had just broken up with a guy. And it seemed like she broke up with one guy and fell for another about every five minutes.

"Pete is history? When?" Marilee demanded. "You didn't say anything to me on the phone last night."

"I didn't see him macking with Krissy Arzt last night," Karly said. "That was behind the gym at lunch today."

"That is so rotten!"

"I felt hurt for about, oh, two seconds. I'm totally over it. I figure they deserve each other. And Brian Krowski has started to get really cute lately."

"Brian 'Barfboy' Krowski?" Marilee marveled. "He used to upchuck like every day on the playground."

"That was when you guys were in the third grade," Karly reminded Marilee. "He had some kind of food allergy. He outgrew it."

Marilee made a face. "Yeah, but how could you ever kiss a guy whose nickname used to be Barfboy?"

"You should see him; you'd understand." Karly hit Marilee with a pillow. "How's your dad doing? I haven't seen him in like forever."

"Dad is . . . Dad." Marilee sighed. "This week's get-rich-quick scheme was catfish stink bait with a chili-and-turkey-liver base."

Karly wrinkled her nose. "*So* nasty."

Marilee nodded. "Plus, it didn't catch any fish."

Karly lay on her stomach and folded her arms under her head. "I don't know why he doesn't open a nursery service. He's so amazing with plants."

Marilee shrugged. She never bad-mouthed her dad, not even to Karly. For one thing, she loved him too much. And for another, well, he was her dad, even if he wasn't perfect. Even if he was terrible with money. Even if he had used money they'd set aside for bills to buy the ingredients for his special stink bait.

Karly could read Marilee's discomfort just by looking at her friend's face, so she changed the subject. "Did you talk to Adam about getting him to write a song for you?"

"Uh, not exactly."

"Look, all you do is open your mouth and you say, 'Adam, so what if you've turned into a hunk of burning love? I'm ignoring that because I need to talk to you without thinking about how much I want you to kiss me. So what I want to know is—' "

She was interrupted by the sound of a sharp rap at the front door.

"Hey, Marilee! You here?" a voice called.

Adam. It gave Marilee a thrill just to hear his voice.

"Adam's here, Marilee," Grammy called.

"Perfect!" Karly exclaimed. "Here's your chance. As future chief of the fire department of the city of Carter, Louisiana, I order you to march out there and ask him—"

"No way!" Marilee started to protest, but Karly was already dragging her out the door of her room.

Adam stood there, looking impossibly cute, talking to Grammy.

"Hey, Marilee," he said. "How you doing, Karly?"

"Great," Karly replied. "Hey, I just remembered. Grammy and I have to talk. In private."

Marilee shot Karly a look.

"Gosh, that would mean you two would have to talk with each other," Karly continued blithely.

"You don't have to leave, you know," Marilee told them both, suddenly feeling very shy.

"Ah, but we do," said Karly.

Grammy smiled. "Now, give me a kiss, sugar."

Marilee hugged them both and watched them get into Grammy's pickup truck. Karly stuck her body halfway out the window to wave as Grammy drove away.

"Uh, want to go outside and sit in the Big Room?" Marilee asked Adam.

"Excellent suggestion," Adam replied, affecting a British accent. "I do so adore the green carpeting."

Marilee grinned. "You're insane, you know that?"

"I prefer to think of myself as eccentric."

They went outside and settled down in the plastic lawn chairs. Almost instantly two dogs and five cats came loping around from the other side of the trailer, meowing and barking happily. The big black and white stray cat with the docked tail, which Marilee had named Dog because he acted more like a dog than a cat, jumped into Marilee's lap. She stroked him and raised her face to the sun.

"Mmm, that feels great," she rhapsodized. "I'm picturing myself at some exotic beach resort that costs five thousand dollars a day. Why, my designer bathing suit alone costs that much. And the sunscreen, too. And tonight I'm dining with the Duke and Duchess of Muckamuck."

"Oh, I do adore the Muckamucks," Adam said in his affected voice. "What will Cook be serving, pheasant?"

"Sssh! There are *animals* around. We'll eat vegetarian," Marilee responded. "But I plan to wear my tiara. And then go dancing with my rock star boyfriend."

"Ah yes, the infamous Buzz Cut," Adam invented. "Winner of seven thousand MTV Music Awards."

"It's so annoying when all his little fans beg for his autograph," Marilee said, sighing dramatically.

"That's your idea of a good time, huh?" Adam asked, back to his own voice.

"Sounds okay."

"But it's all such a waste. And you've got too much talent to waste your life," Adam told her earnestly. "And you're smart—"

And beautiful, Marilee willed him to say. *Say I'm beautiful. Please.*

"And you're going to be a world-class photographer one day," Adam concluded. "World-class."

Marilee sighed.

Well, at least he believes in me, she thought. *Even if kissing me is the furthest thing from his mind.*

"Actually, the reason I asked you to come over has to do with my photography," Marilee began. "You know I told you about the Y.A.A. contest—"

"You could win it, you know."

She smiled at him. "How come you believe in me more than I believe in me?"

"How come you were the only person who heard my original tunes for an entire year before I got up the nerve to play them for anyone else?"

" 'Cuz you trusted me," Marilee said.

"Yeah," Adam agreed. "Actually, I have terrific news. About my music."

"I wanted to talk to you about your music, too," Marilee said. "See, the Y.A.A.—"

"Listen, I'm like bursting here, Marilee. I've got to tell you this."

Marilee's heart leaped.

Ms. Pfeffer beat me to it, she reasoned quickly, *and asked him if he'd write me a song for the Y.A.A. Thank you, thank you, Ms. Pfeffer. Thank you for making this easy.*

She swore to herself that when she went back into the trailer, she would write her teacher a thank-you note.

Marilee grinned at him. "I hate it when people bust their guts in the Big Room. It's so . . . messy. So?"

"I've got a great songwriting gig coming up. And I am so jazzed about this, Marilee."

"Me, too," she said giddily. She was so excited that she jumped up and pulled him out of his plastic chair, twirling him in a circle. "I'm so happy."

"How can you be happy when you don't know what it is?"

"I can guess," Marilee said.

"I'm impressed," Adam said. "Ladies and gentlemen, not only can she take incredible photographs, she can also see into the future."

"Right," Marilee teased. "I see . . . an original song."

"Songs."

"I only need—" Marilee stopped herself. A bad feeling began to creep up her neck. "What do you mean, songs?"

"The ones Olivia asked me to write," Adam explained. "Olivia and her family are having a twenty-fifth anniversary party for her parents and I'm supposed to write like eight songs for the score to this video presentation. Originals. Fifty bucks a tune. *Fifty bucks.* That's four hundred dollars, Marilee. For doing the thing I love to do more than anything else in the world!"

Marilee's heart sank. She looked down at Dog so Adam wouldn't see the hurt in her eyes.

"That's really great, Adam," she said finally. And it was true. She was happy for him, in a way, to be getting paid to write songs. Even if it meant he wouldn't have time to work on her project.

But do they have to be for Olivia's family?

"When I get paid, I'm buying you more film than you can use in this lifetime," he promised her.

She forced herself to look up and smile. "You don't have to do that."

"How about what you can use this year, then?"

"That's really nice of you, Adam."

His eyes searched hers. "What's wrong?"

"Nothing."

"Marilee, you can't fool me. Something's wrong. Oh, I get it. It's because it's for Livy and her family."

"Adam, she's hateful to me."

"It's a job, Marilee. My first real songwriting job."

"I know."

He frowned. "I think there's something you're not telling me. What did you want to talk about, anyhow?"

There were so many things she wanted to say to him.

But for her to say any of them—especially to ask him to write a song for her for free, when *Livy* was paying him so much money to do the same thing—was impossible.

More than impossible. Utterly, totally hopeless.

So she changed the subject, and then they played with the animals, laughing when Dog the cat chased down a Frisbee. But even though she was with Adam and the animals she loved so much, Marilee felt very alone.

Chapter

4

"Morning, sweetie, I fed the animals!" Marilee's father called to her as she padded sleepily from her room at the back of the trailer.

"Thanks, Daddy," Marilee told him, going to pour herself some coffee. "Good book?"

Mr. Ellis was on the couch, reading *How to Make Your Second Million*. "Great. Cuz I already gave up on the first. It's a joke. Get it?"

"Got it, Daddy."

Her father got up. "Want me to make you some eggs? I think Grammy left some in the—"

"I'm not hungry, Daddy. Thanks."

He sat back down. "What did you do last night? The Calhouns kept me up at the house until after ten."

"I studied for history," Marilee said. "I tried to call Grammy but the phone wasn't working. You did pay the phone bill, didn't you, Daddy?"

Her father scratched his chin. "It might have slipped my mind, sweetie. Mrs. Calhoun had me running around—"

"Do we have enough money?" Marilee asked softly.

"Today we do," her father said brightly. "I got a bonus for fixing her cellar stairs. It's Saturday, we'll pay the bill first thing Monday morning. "We can always use the Calhouns' phone. All this is gonna change. I got this new idea that's a surefire winner. Our ship is gonna come in and then, hoo-boy, we'll be in the chip."

Marilee sipped her coffee as her father gazed at her with hopeful eyes. His last idea was catfish bait.

He took her gently by the shoulders. "I swear it, Marilee, someday you'll be living in a house bigger than the Calhouns'. It's what you deserve. That's my biggest goal in life. I mean it."

Marilee nodded. She'd heard this from her father so many times that it pained her to hear it again. But how do you tell your own father that he's not making the most of what he has, of the wonderful skills and qualities that made him who he was?

She didn't know. So she changed the subject.

"What are you cooking?" Something toma-toey and spicy, was bubbling on the stove.

"Million number two," her father said eagerly. He went to the pot and gave it a stir. "Ketchup."

"Ketchup?" Marilee echoed.

"Gourmet ketchup," Mr. Ellis explained. "For the yuppies to put on their gourmet buffalo burgers and all."

He put a finger into the pot, then lifted it to his lips. "Might need more garlic. You want to try it?"

Marilee shook her head and reached for a slice of toast. "Not before breakfast, thanks."

Mr. Ellis laughed. "I know what you're thinking. My old man again, with yet another scheme. Isn't that right?"

Marilee smiled. Her father was who he was. He wasn't going to change.

In one way, it was sweet. Her father was like a little kid with his ideas that never worked. Before bait, there was an automatic toilet-seat putter-downer that didn't work. He never gave up.

In another way, though, it was sad. She knew how wonderful her father was with plants—he had a real talent. But whenever she or Grammy reminded him of that, he turned them down flat. Horticulturalists didn't make the big money.

He didn't used to be like this, Marilee recalled. *Back in Carter, he used to talk about going to night school to study horticulture. And he'd draw plans for the most beautiful gardens. But when he couldn't find another job there, and we had to move to Overton, it was like even those dreams disappeared.*

"I can hear those wheels of yours turning, Marilee," her father said as he stirred his ketchup. "But I'm telling you, sweetie, this time is it."

Marilee took a deep breath and screwed up her courage.

"Daddy, you're so talented with gardens and plants. You could get a real job with a real company, with benefits. And go to the community college at night for horticulture. And we could move into a real—"

"Come on, sweetie. If I had a real job with a real company, I wouldn't have any free time to invent the thing that's going to make our fortune, now would I?"

"Could you make our fortune after work, maybe?"

Mr. Ellis laughed.

"When I succeed, Daddy," Marilee declared, "it'll be because I worked for it."

He smiled at her. "Big-time photographer, right? I'll be proud of you."

She closed her eyes and tried to imagine a cover of *National Geographic,* a cover with a photo on it that she had taken. And then she imagined taking that photograph, maybe from a tree stand someplace in Africa, Adam with her, cheering her on.

It was such a beautiful thought that she wanted to think it forever.

*　　*　　*

Later that morning Marilee pushed the doorbell to the Calhoun mansion, hoping against hope that Elenora, the housekeeper, would answer the door.

Hope failed her. Mrs. Calhoun answered.

Marilee would never have been ringing Mrs. Calhoun's doorbell if their phone bill had been paid on time. But she really had to call the Overton Public Library to see if they had a book she needed for her Y.A.A. project. Maybe her father would be able to pick it up for her later.

"Hello, Marilee," Mrs. Calhoun said. "What brings you here so early?"

"I'd like to use the phone," Marilee said, mustering all her courage. "Ours is . . . out."

"Of course," Mrs. Calhoun said. She was dressed in khakis and a perfect white shirt, her hair covered with a straw hat and her hands covered in gardening gloves. "I was just overseeing my autumn flower beds. Your father prepared them wonderfully. Of course you may use the phone, Marilee. I'm glad you're here, actually. I wanted to talk to you. Come back to the formal gardens when you're done, won't you?"

"Yes, ma'am," Marilee said.

Her heart began to pound. What could Mrs. Calhoun possibly want to see her about? Had one of the dogs torn up her flower beds? But that would be impossible; Marilee was certain that they couldn't get over the fence to the Calhouns' main yard.

Maybe she's going to fire my father, Marilee thought, her mind panicking. *And she wants to warn me first. But why?*

Marilee spotted a phone on a side table and used it to call the library. The book she wanted had been taken out.

Hanging over the telephone table she noticed something: a framed photograph of the Calhoun house she had taken last winter, right after a freezing rainstorm. The storm had knocked out power for two days, but the mansion looked like a fairy-tale castle shimmering in icicles.

Marilee had given it to the Calhouns as a Christmas present.

Huh. So Mrs. Calhoun liked it. She'd had it framed and hung it on the wall. It was the first time Marilee had seen one of her photos professionally framed and hung in someone's home.

It was kind of thrilling, actually.

Marilee went outside to the formal gardens, where Mrs. Calhoun was bent over some late-blooming petunias.

"Hi," Marilee said shyly. "You wanted to talk to me?"

Mrs. Calhoun stood up and stretched her back. "These petunias are lovely," she said. "You father does excellent work. He could run a landscaping and horticultural business if he ever wanted to."

I know, Marilee thought.

"My dad has a lot of abilities," Marilee said cautiously.

Mrs. Calhoun went and sat on a floral-cushioned outdoor settee, her hands folded primly in her lap. "Have a seat, Marilee."

Marilee sat on a little chair nearby.

"My sweet little niece, Logan, a truly darling child, is coming to visit from Baton Rouge. And tomorrow, Sunday, we're giving a lovely garden party for her."

Marilee nodded. Her father had been grumbling for days about all the extra hours Mrs. Calhoun had him putting in to get ready for some shindig for some little kid.

"We're expecting about fifty people," Mrs. Calhoun went on. "I'm concerned we may not have enough help. Would you be interested in helping out? Starting, at say, three? I'll pay you fifteen dollars an hour. Cash, of course."

Marilee thought quickly. She was working the Sunday brunch shift at Hava Java, but that was over at two. She could easily be back home and changed for the party by three. Fifteen dollars an hour was fantastic pay. It would buy a lot of food for the animals. Or film for her.

"I'll be here," Marilee promised.

"Wonderful." Mrs. Calhoun stood up. "You'll like Logan. She's very sweet."

Marilee smiled and nodded her agreement, as she pictured an angelic-looking ten-year-old in lace who took the hired help totally for granted.

Mrs. Calhoun stood up. "Well, I'm glad this will work out for you. And please wear something long-sleeved and black, Marilee. Clean and pressed. I don't require uniforms but I will provide you with a white apron to match that of the others."

That was it. Mrs. Calhoun turned her attention back to her gardening.

No "Good-bye, Marilee." No "Thank you for bailing me out, Marilee."

If I ever get rich I'll never take people for granted, Marilee swore to herself as she turned to go back to the trailer. *Not even if they were as cold as Olivia Fairmont.*

Well, maybe I'd be mean to Olivia Fairmont for fifteen minutes, she amended as got to the front door. *Just to see how it feels.*

She got home, rolled around on the grass with the animals for a while, then went into her bedroom and shut the door. She picked up the framed photo of her mother. Forever twenty-three years old in the picture. Forever young and smiling and perfect.

"Only that isn't real life, Mom, is it?" she whispered. "In real life, the phone bill doesn't always get paid. Kids make fun of you because you can't shop where they shop. And Livy is making Adam smile in a way that I can't."

Marilee set the photo down and lay on her bed.

I wish I were rich like Livy.

She stopped herself. No. No way. She was not going to engage in a pity party of one. What was the point? Even photographers for *National Geographic* didn't get rich. They got their rewards in other ways. And she would not trade her life for Livy Fairmont's any day of the week.

Okay, how about if I get to be me and *get to be a photographer for* National Geographic and *I get to be rich?*

That thought was so funny to her that it made her laugh out loud.

Chapter

5

"*You* look wonderful," Karly assured Marilee on Sunday afternoon.

"You think?" Marilee seemed doubtful. She moved around in front of the mirror on her bedroom wall, trying to catch her reflection.

It hadn't been easy putting together the right outfit. Her own nice black top was sleeveless, so she'd borrowed her dad's black sweater. It was huge on her, plus there was a tiny hole under the left arm. Still, if she didn't lift that arm, it was more than passable.

She didn't own black pants that weren't jeans, either. But Grammy had bought her a black skirt over the summer. It was far too big on her, but she and Karly pinned it at the waist so it would stay up. Then they covered the safety pins by pulling the sweater down.

It worked . . . if she didn't move too abruptly.

"If I were Freddy Prinze Junior, I'd ask you out," Karly told her after checking her over.

"The question is, would he go out with the hired help? I'm a waitress at Logan's party, remember?"

"Please." Karly sniffed. "Didn't Prince Charming still love Cinderella after she returned to her former life?"

"You see a Prince Charming with character."

"Exactly," Karly agreed. "No shallow princes allowed."

"You sure you're going to be okay by yourself?"

Karly pointed to her open geometry book. Karly was home-schooled, and her mom, who taught her, was a bit of a slave driver. "Trust me"— she made a face—"this will keep me more than occupied. And I rented a great movie for later."

"Don't forget to feed the cats. Dog only likes Starkist tuna. I can't believe you want to watch a video with me here instead of going out tonight with Barfboy."

"Who? Old news. You really need to keep up. I met—"

A knock on the door interrupted Karly.

"Come in!" Marilee called.

Her father opened the door. "Well, sweetie, how does your old man look?"

Marilee and Karly looked at him in astonishment.

"Mr. Ellis," Karly said, "if there's a sudden flood this afternoon, you'll be the most popular man at the party."

Mr. Ellis laughed good-naturedly. He was working at the party, too, and the only tux he could rent had pants that barely came down to the middle of his ankles.

"You clean up nice, Daddy," Marilee teased lightly. "Even in high-waters, you'll be the handsomest guy at the party."

"Marilee," Mr. Ellis said, "I forgot to give you this. Adam dropped it off while you were at Hava Java."

He handed her a folded piece of notebook paper that had MARILEE on the front in big, block letters.

Marilee—
Brain-dead me forgot you were doing brunch shift at Hava Java. I feel really bad that you didn't get to tell me whatever it was you wanted to tell me the other day. Your dad said you're going to Grammy's after work, so I guess I won't get to talk to you until school tomorrow. I'm hoping what you were going to tell me about is what you decided to do for the Y.A.A. contest. Keep clicking those photos! Talk to you tomorrow.

—Adam

No "love." No "I'll miss you." Just "Adam."

Marilee shoved the note into her pocket. "Why did you tell him I was going to Grammy's, Daddy?"

"I wasn't about to tell him you were spending the afternoon playin' servant to those rich patoots." He cocked his head in the direction of the Calhoun house.

He has a point, Marilee thought. *After all, I didn't tell Adam I was working at this party. Especially now that he's writing songs for one of those rich patoots, Livy Fairmont.*

Marilee and the four other women who were working the Calhoun party had white pinafore-style aprons tied over their black clothing. The words "Impeccable Taste" were embroidered near their right shoulders.

Arnold Akin, owner of Impeccable Taste, was catering the party. And he was, to put it mildly, extremely fussy. For the past hour he'd alternately issued orders to the kitchen staff and then complained about how those orders were being executed.

The lobster pâté was not supposed to be on the same tray as the toast points, and where was the watercress garnish, anyway? What imbecile had just thrown endive onto the plate like that? He'd specifically left a diagram of how it should be arranged like a giant flower.

Et cetera, et cetera, et cetera.

"Ladies," Akin was saying now, "the doilies under the smoked salmon are crooked. Do the tray over. Quickly!" He clapped his hands to emphasize his point.

Marilee and one of the other workers, a pasty-skinned, heavyset young woman named Charma, traded looks as they began to remove the smoked salmon from the tray.

"You ever work for Akin before?" Charma asked Marilee, her voice low.

Marilee shook her head.

"Well, soon you'll be fixin' to call him Mister Oh-My-Akin-Back. The man's the worst boss in history."

Marilee lined the tray with new paper doilies, careful to make sure they were perfectly centered. "I just think it's a little gross to do all this for some little kid," she said. "I mean, I know adults will be at this party, but really, kids don't eat pâté and smoked salmon and—"

"What little kid?" Charma asked, confused.

"That girl, Logan. Who this party is for. I guess she's still upstairs getting her hair brushed by the hair brusher. Or getting her shoes shined by the—"

"She ain't no little kid," Charma interrupted. "She's—"

"Hello," said a melodious female voice behind them.

Marilee turned around.

There stood a slender girl about Marilee's age. Her glossy dark hair was cut into a gorgeous bob that fell just past her chin. She wore a simple, but very elegant, long dress and a single strand of tiny pearls.

"I'm Logan Calhoun," the girl said, holding a graceful hand out to Marilee, then to Charma.

Marilee shook it numbly and mumbled her own name. She'd been so *sure* that Mrs. Calhoun had said her niece was a child.

"Thanks for all your help with my party," Logan said. "I really appreciate it."

"You're welcome," Marilee said, unable to think of anything else to say.

Charma didn't bother to respond. She just carried the tray of smoked salmon into the dining room, and Marilee followed with another tray.

"Look at all this food," Logan said, trailing Marilee. "My aunt claimed this was going to be just a simple little garden party."

"This *is* her concept of 'simple,' " Marilee said before she could stop herself.

Logan laughed. "You're right. You'd think I'd know that by now." She plucked a cucumber slice from a tray and nibbled it daintily. "So, do you live in Overton?"

"No," Marilee lied. "In Carter, about a half hour from here." She was not about to confide in Logan Calhoun that she resided in a mobile home at the edge of the Calhoun estate. It was too embarrassing.

"Oh, well then, I guess you wouldn't know any of my friends who go to Overton High," Logan said.

"Logan?" a girlish voice squealed.

Marilee shut her eyes.

"Livy Fairmont!" Logan exclaimed. "What a surprise. I thought you said you'd be out of town. But you came!"

It couldn't be.

But it was.

Chapter

6

Marilee tried not to watch as Livy and Logan hugged warmly, laughing and jabbering about how much they had missed each other and how cute the other one looked and—

Then Livy noticed Marilee.

"Marilee?" Livy asked, sounding incredulous. "What are *you* doing here?"

"Slumming it," Marilee said sweetly. She couldn't help herself, even though she knew it was not professional. Still, it was better than saying something nasty.

"Well, how classic!" Livy laughed. Bree, who'd just joined her, starting laughing, too. Marilee turned away and kept working.

Logan looked confused. "You know each other?"

"Well, we don't exactly *hang out*," Olivia replied, trading eye rolls with Bree, "but Overton isn't that big."

Logan cocked her head at Marilee. "But I thought you said you lived in . . . what was the name again?"

"She lives—" Olivia began, then whispered the rest it into Logan's ear.

Marilee could just imagine what Olivia was telling her. Some of it truth and some of it lies.

"Trailer trash. She lives right here on your aunt's property. In a mobile home. They don't even have a bathroom. They use an outhouse in the woods."

Marilee pretended that she'd just thought of something, and headed for the place farthest from Livy and Bree and Logan that she could imagine. The kitchen.

Mr. Akin awaited her there. "Take that tray out to the garden, Miss Ellis." He motioned at a tray of crab cakes. "And smile. Sour faces make for sour service."

She scowled. She wasn't getting paid to smile.

Then she stopped herself.

She *was* getting paid to smile, she realized. Mrs. Calhoun was paying her. And no matter how much she didn't want to be serving at a party where Livy and Bree were invited guests, she, Marilee Ellis, was not a quitter.

If she was hired to do a job, she did it right. She wasn't going to let those girls make her feel bad about herself. No way. She was going to do her job.

With a smile on her face.

Marilee took a deep breath, put on her best waitress smile, and then went to work serving.

"Would you care for a crab cake?" she asked a group of people gathered near the flower beds. She moved professionally and confidently from that group to another to another to another, saying the same thing over and over, smiling but not making eye contact.

When her tray emptied, Mr. Akin immediately replaced it with a tray of cajun shrimp.

The late-afternoon sun was warm, and Marilee began to perspire. Some flyaway hair came loose from her ponytail, but she was working too hard and diligently to do anything about it.

"Would you care for some cajun shrimp? Would you care for some—"

"I could take that sweater into the house for you, if you'd like," Logan offered, coming over to Marilee.

"I'm fine," Marilee said.

"It's just that you look like you're really warm, carrying all those trays out here," Logan explained.

Marilee got an instant picture in her mind of Logan and Livy hugging and whispering about her. Maybe Livy had even sent Logan up to come over to her. So they could all laugh at Marilee some more.

No, she was not going to be part of that game.

"Gee, I'd love to give you my sweater," Marilee said, "except I have to wear black, and the bra I have on underneath is kind of white."

Logan smiled apologetically. "Sorry, I just figured you had a shirt on under the——"

"Would you like a cajun shrimp?"

"No, thanks. Listen, Marilee, I was wondering if——"

"Logan!" Olivia called from the sliding glass doors. "Come on in and meet my boyfriend. He finally got here."

"Excuse me," Logan told Marilee. "I have to go meet Olivia's latest, though knowing Livy's track record, I don't envy the guy for one——"

"Never mind, I brought him out," Olivia shouted, rushing over to Logan, hand in hand with her new boyfriend.

Hand in hand with Adam.

Adam?

Boyfriend?

When he saw Marilee, he looked amazed.

"What are you doing here?" they asked each other at exactly the same moment.

"I know exactly what he's doing here," Olivia said, taking Adam's arm proprietarily.

"Marilee——" Adam began.

But she had already moved away toward the formal gardens, offering cajun shrimp to anyone in sight.

"Marilee." Adam came up behind her. She felt his hand on her shoulder.

She shook it off. "I'm working. Please. Please leave me alone."

"But your father told me you were going to Grammy's—"

"What difference does it make?"

"A lot," he said earnestly. "Come on, I never would have come if I had known you were going to be serving—"

"She introduced you as her boy—"

"Miss Ellis, you are not here to socialize with the guests," Mr. Akin rushed over, shouting. "Clear off those empty trays, pronto."

"I'm the one who talked to her, sir," Adam said firmly. "And I'm not quite through yet." He reached for Marilee's arm again.

"Yes, you are," Marilee said. "Adam, please. Just go back to your girlfriend. And leave me alone."

"But, Marilee, you—"

"The empty trays, Miss Ellis?" Mr. Akin repeated.

Wordlessly, Marilee began to load her arms with the empty silver trays, her load getting heavier and heavier. She didn't know where Adam had gone and she wasn't going to think about it. Because if she did, she'd lose it.

Olivia's boyfriend.

Forget it, she told herself. *Or save it and cry on*

Karly's shoulder later. But not now. You are a professional at whatever you are hired to do.

She was being paid to do a job and she was going to do it right. She didn't care if some of these people never worked a day in their entire lives, she would always work hard for what she had, and—

"Watch out!" someone yelled as the load of trays in Marilee's arms began to topple.

Instinctively she grabbed at the falling trays. As she did, she felt the safety pin holding up her skirt snap.

The trays tumbled to the ground.

And so did her skirt.

From the front, she was covered by her apron. But from the rear, there was just Marilee in her cotton panties.

Someone gasped.

Other than that, there was total silence.

Then, from behind her, came the familiar sound of Bree's braying laugh.

Five hours later, Marilee trudged through the door of their trailer. Grammy was sitting on the couch doing a crossword puzzle and watching TV. When she saw her granddaughter's expression, she was instantly on her feet.

"Marilee? Lord have mercy, what happened?"

Marilee let herself be enveloped in her grandmother's loving arms. She had managed to control herself at the party even after the tray disaster. She'd put on some black pants that Mrs. Estes found for her and went back to work.

She had wanted to run away, to never look back, but she knew that if she ran away, she'd keep running.

No. She didn't give in. She had been hired to work, so she stayed and worked. It didn't matter how much Bree and Livy and Logan laughed at her. Or even if Adam was there as Livy's boyfriend. If she had run away, they'd have won.

If she stayed, she'd win.

But now, in the safety of her own home, she let all her pent-up emotions run free.

"Oh, Grammy, it was horrible," she moaned as her grandmother held her just the way she had when she was little.

And she recounted everything that had happened.

With the trays.

With Livy and Bree and Logan.

With Adam.

"My poor baby," Grammy said soothingly, rocking Marilee in her arms. "You just have to decide you don't give two figs for what those ol' people think, honey."

"But Adam—"

"Honey, except for Karly, Adam Eagleton is your best friend in the world," Grammy reminded her. "Best friends don't go judging each other."

"But he was there with her, Grammy," Marilee went on. "She called him her boyfriend."

"Maybe he is and maybe he isn't," Grammy said. "If I know Adam, he'll sort it all out with you."

"Where did Karly go?" Marilee managed.

"There was a four-alarmer in Graverton," Grammy told Marilee. "Her father knew she'd want to see it, so he sent someone to pick her up. He was right."

Marilee smiled. "Some things never change," she said.

"Thank goodness," the elderly lady agreed. "As for Adam, you think I'm too old to remember what it's like when you fall in love for the first time?"

Marilee blew her nose. "How did you know?"

"I didn't," Grammy confessed. "Until tonight."

"But Adam doesn't love me back," Marilee said, her voice small. "It hurts."

Grammy smiled sadly. "I wish I could take away all your hurts, honey, and make all your dreams come true."

Marilee sat up. "They're not gonna come true, Grammy."

"Don't say that—"

"Why not? It's true."

"You're such a special person, Marilee," her

grandmother said. "And such a wonderful photographer. Why, you could win that photography contest you told me about. A summer at that school of photography—"

"Design," Marilee corrected her. "In Rhode Island. But I'll never win, Grammy."

"Don't go talking like that, Marilee."

"Why not?" Marilee asked, blowing her nose again. "Winning would be like a fairy tale. But my life is not exactly a fairy tale where dreams come true."

"In this life, sweetie, if its going to happen, you have to work hard. I know you can do that. You've done it all your life."

Marilee got up wearily. "I'm tired, Grammy. I'm going to bed."

Marilee had taken a few steps toward her bedroom when her grandmother's voice stopped her.

"Marilee?"

She turned back to her grandmother.

"I wish I could give you the moon with a fence around it, but I can't," Grammy said. She reached into her purse and took something out. "The other day I got home from grocery shopping, and there, in the back of the pickup, was the prettiest thing."

Grammy opened her cupped hands. She held a beautiful, glittery, heart-shaped object. It was like nothing Marilee had ever seen before.

"I thought I'd use it for a paperweight," Grammy went on. "But then I thought, this here thing is as lovely as Marilee. So here it is. For you."

Grammy held it out to her.

Marilee took the rock into her own hands. It felt warm, electric, almost alive. It actually seemed to glow with an eerie light.

"I never saw anything like it," Marilee murmured. "Did your hands feel all tingly when you held this? Maybe it's got poison ivy on it or something."

Grammy shook her head. "Can't recollect that they did. I just thought it was as special as you are. Maybe it will bring you good luck, like wishing on a shooting star."

Impetuously, Marilee hugged her grandmother fiercely. "I love you, Grammy. Thank you."

"Well, then"—Grammy patted Marilee's hand—"go to sleep."

Marilee kissed her grandmother good night, went outside to get Dog the cat so that she could sleep with him, carried him into her room, and got ready for bed.

Then she picked up the glittering rock again. The strangest sensation filled her.

You can be your dream, a voice inside her said.

She closed her hands around the rock, and warm vibrations radiated through her body.

Put it under your pillow and dream your dreams.
You can be your dream. You can be your dream.

Marilee slipped the rock under her pillow, lay down, and closed her eyes. Dog curled up right by her head.

"Sleeping with a rock under my head might mean I have rocks *in* my head," she said aloud, yawning.

Marilee smiled. *I wish I were rich*, she thought. *So rich that I could do whatever I wanted and no one could ever humiliate me again and Adam would love me and not Olivia.*

With that thought on her lips and the strange, glittering, heart-shaped object under her pillow, Marilee fell asleep.

Chapter

7

"Good morning, New Orleans!" chortled "Weird" Willie Williams, New Orleans's reigning radio "shock jock," to whom Mr. Ellis was addicted.

Marilee opened her eyes. She detested Weird Willie. All he did was make fun of people and crack stupid, crude jokes. But her father found him hilarious, which is why he was always on first thing in the morning.

"You've got a scorcher this morning, New Orleans," Weird Willie went on as Dog the cat jumped off the bed and scampered into the kitchen. "Speaking of scorchers, I've got Lyla Childs, star of the hit movie *Love Ties*, with me in the studio. And I'm telling you, this girl is hot to trot!"

Marilee groaned and put her pillow over her head. Her cheek hit something hard—the glittering heart-shaped rock Grammy had given her the day before.

She picked it up.

It was strange. She got the same tingly feeling as when she'd held the Loverock last night.

Loverock. Funny. It had just come to her. But it was a perfect name for it, really. It was heart-shaped. And Grammy had certainly given it to her out of love.

Marilee set the object on her nightstand. Keeping the pillow over her head wasn't going to make getting ready to go to school happen more quickly.

"It's a big day in the Big Easy," Weird Willie went on. "Everyone in bayou country has got that Lotto fever. So all you stupid suckers out there with a dollar and a dream, drive your pickups and your crappy vintage Yugos down to the nearest convenience store and donate your bucks to the government. Better yet, why don't you just get L-O-S-E-R tattooed on your forehead, cuz you got as much chance of winning the Lotto as you have of getting invited to tea by the governor of Louisiana. Say hello to all the losers out there, lovely Lyla!"

"Hello, Losers!" a breathy female voice cooed.

"Daddy, turn down the radio, please!"

Weird Willie's voice dropped to a dull roar.

"Thank you, Daddy," Marilee called. "You decent?"

"Some folks don't think so," her father joked. "But I have my pants on. Listen, before I left that fancy party yesterday, Logan Calhoun gave me a note to give to you."

Marilee felt sick to her stomach. *Right. Logan and Livy are best friends. That note is something to make fun of me. Why should I give her the satisfaction?*

"Toss it, Daddy," Marilee called.

Marilee pulled on some clothes, went outside the trailer, changed the water for the dogs and cats, and put fresh pellets in the rabbit hutch. The dogs and cats brushed against her legs gratefully as she fed them. She threw Dog the Frisbee a couple of times.

At least that horrible party paid me enough money so I can buy food for these guys for a while, she thought.

Marilee could hear Weird Willie and Lyla prattling on through the window of the mobile home. Willie was telling people to join him at Monument Square in New Orleans at noontime, where he'd be throwing a Lotto Suckers party.

"Give me your dollars," Willie was saying. "I'll put 'em to good use!"

He's mean, Marilee thought. *The Lotto gives those people a little hope for a little while. Hope can change a person, because without hope you're—*

Suddenly an idea came to her.

Maybe even a really *good* idea.

Marilee ran into the trailer and threw her school clothes on. She gulped down a cup of coffee and grabbed a slice of toast. Then, quickly, she gathered up her books and the camera she had borrowed from school, and kissed her father on the cheek as she flew out the door.

"You sure are anxious to catch that school bus," he called after her.

"No bus, Daddy," she called. "See you later!"

If I run, I can get fifteen minutes at the Two/Five, she thought as she jogged. *I can pay the phone bill and still have time to do what I need to do.*

The suckers, Weird Willie called them.

Only they aren't suckers, Marilee thought. *They're just people with dreams.*

She got to the Two/Five store twenty minutes later and her heart leaped as she saw a long line of people snaking out the door, waiting to buy Lotto tickets.

There were people of every conceivable size and shape, age and color. There were housewives and old men, matrons and laborers, housekeepers and college students.

Right in Overton. Well-to-do Overton. Dozens of people, full of dreams.

Grammy's right, Marilee thought. *The best dreams are the ones you work hard to achieve. But if you want to take a one-in-a-zillion chance on a fan-*

tasy, and all it costs you is a dollar, there's nothing wrong with that, either.

Unless you use the food money or the electric bill money or the—

She forced her mind to shut up for a while. She didn't want to analyze. She wanted to get to work.

Phone bill first, she thought.

"Excuse me, excuse me," she said to the line of people as she tried to wind her way inside.

"Yo, Lotto Maniac Girl, no cuttin'!" a young white guy with dreadlocks and baggy jeans objected. His T-shirt read MARLEY in hand-printed letters.

"I need to pay my phone bill," Marilee explained.

"Oh, cool," the guy said, nodding. "No problem, then." He made space for her to get through the line.

"Excuse me, excuse me," Marilee repeated, turning sideways. There were nearly as many people inside the store as outside. All of them were lined up to see a single overworked clerk selling Lotto tickets.

Fortunately, another clerk was handling all the other store business, so Marilee got into that much shorter line to pay her phone bill. Then she worked her way back through the crowd, anxious to get outside where she could take some photos in the natural morning light.

"Yo! Lotto Maniac Girl, pay your phone bill?" someone called.

It was the white kid with the dreadlocks again.

"It's 'Marilee.' And, yeah, I did." Marilee pulled out her camera. "Thanks for letting me through."

"No problem, mon," he replied, suddenly putting on a Jamaican accent. " 'Nuff respect, mon."

Marilee began to shoot a series of rapid photos of him.

"Hey, what're you doing?" he objected, his accent gone.

"You mind?" Marilee clicked off some more shots, and then as unobtrusively as possible, took photos of others in the line who hadn't noticed her presence.

"Not if you're gonna make me a star. The name is Marley. I play reggae." He beamed into Marilee's camera.

"You don't live around here, do you?" Marilee asked as the power drive of her camera whirred.

"In St. Charles Parish," Marley said. "There's teacher conferences at my school today. My uncle owns Hava Java. He said he has this waitress who's always late after school, so he asked me if I could work there today, and I need the bread, so—"

Marilee laughed.

"What's so funny?" Marley asked.

"I'm the waitress."

Marley grinned. "No kidding? You working later?"

Marilee clicked off some more shots and nodded.

"Hey, not to worry," Marley said. "I'm not into this whole capitalist system thing, anyway." He shot her the peace sign. "One love, mon."

Marilee said she'd see him later and moved around, clicking away. The more photos she took, the more excited she got.

This would be the basis of her Y.A.A. entry. Real people, real dreams. Far better than animals. As for the multimedia part, she could write her own poetry and record it, and maybe she'd put some music behind that.

So what if it wasn't an original song from Adam? She could do it herself.

Marilee looked at her watch. She was going to be late for school. She'd have to run three-quarters of a mile, or catch the bus down Main Street, or—

"Yo, Lotto Maniac Girl!"

Marilee stuffed her camera in her knapsack as Marley approached her. "Can't talk, late for school, gotta run."

"Where?"

"Overton High."

"I'll drive you," Marley offered.

"Oh no, sorry, I don't get into strange guys' cars," Marilee said, backing away. "Thanks, anyway."

"Well, take this, then." He pulled out a lottery ticket and handed it to her.

"A Lotto ticket? Why?"

Marley shrugged. "Who knows? Call it a random act of kindness. Anyway, I'm not takin' it back. You don't want it, give it away. See you at Hava Java, Lotto Maniac Girl."

"Thanks," Marilee said gratefully. It was nice to see someone doing something nice for no reason. She thrust the Lotto ticket into her pocket and took off toward school.

She was so excited about her idea for the Y.A.A. contest that she wasn't even thinking about who'd be waiting for her once she got there.

"You're late, Marilee," Ms. Booker said when Marilee ran breathlessly into her American history class.

"I know, I'm sorry," Marilee panted.

"Just take a seat," the teacher said, then continued her lecture on Abraham Lincoln and the Gettysburg Address.

Marilee slid into her usual seat near the back. She looked down at her desk.

It was covered with safety pins.

From across the room, she heard Olivia and Bree's snorts. Then more laughter from behind her. Two other girls and two guys, all part of their clique, were smirking.

Which meant Olivia and Bree had told everyone.

Marilee's face burned, but she was not going to let them win.

Let them laugh, Marilee thought. *I wouldn't trade personalities with them for all the money in the world.*

When class ended, she gathered up her books, walked past Bree and Livy with her head held high, and started for her locker.

"Marilee! Hey, Marilee, wait up!" Adam called.

No, not Adam. Not yet. She couldn't face him.

"I'm in a hurry," she said when he'd caught up with her.

"No, you're not, you're avoiding me. Because of the party," he said, striding down the hall beside her.

"Listen, Adam, hard as you might find this to believe, I've got other things on my mind, okay?" She stopped at her locker and spun the combination on her lock, catching the hurt on his face as she yanked her locker open.

"Last I heard, we were still best friends," Adam said quietly. "Or has that changed?"

"Everything has changed, that's pretty obvious. If you're going to waste time hanging around with Livy Fairmont." Marilee got out her math book and pushed her locker shut.

"Hey, Marilee, catch!" someone yelled, and threw a safety pin at her.

Adam picked it up from the floor, his face a mask of fury. He was about to throw the safety pin back at the kid when Marilee stopped him. "Don't bother."

"But —"

"I said, don't bother."

"Marilee—"

"Look, Adam, it's perfectly okay," Marilee lied. "People change. I can deal with it. Besides, I met this new guy. Marley."

It was the first name that had popped into her head.

"You did?" Adam asked.

"He's a musician, too. Reggae. I'm meeting him later."

Adam ran a hand through his hair. "So, what does that mean about us, then?"

She forced herself to look at him. "Why don't you ask Livy that?" she said softly. And then she turned and walked away so that he wouldn't see the tears in her eyes.

"Look at this, sweetie!" Marilee's father called to her as she turned the volume up on their TV.

It was ten o'clock that night. Marilee hadn't run into Marley at Hava Java after school. In fact, he hadn't shown up, and his uncle complained to Marilee about how unreliable he was.

"Abducted by aliens," Marilee had joked with Mr. Wilson. He didn't laugh.

"Marilee!" her dad called again.

She sighed, sat up, and padded into the living room. She'd been lying on her bed, her head filled with Adam. She hadn't even been able to discuss what had happened with Karly because Karly hadn't been home when Marilee called after work. Her heart was just so sad. She couldn't imagine her life without Adam.

"What is it, Daddy?"

"Ten o'clock news. The Lotto jackpot is up to twenty million. They're about to call the numbers."

"So? It's not like you have a ticket—"

Then Marilee realized her father was clutching not one Lotto ticket in his hands, but five.

"You spent our money on *those?*"

"Hey, someone's got to win, sweetie," he pointed out.

"Your odds of getting hit by lightning are a whole lot better," Marilee said. "One ticket, maybe. But five?"

"Shhh." Her father turned the volume up on the TV.

"This is Timber Lee," the young female news anchor for the local ABC affiliate said. "About to bring you, live, in just a few moments, the drawing from Baton Rouge of the Louisiana Lotto, in which the Lucky ticket will win a twenty-million-dollar jackpot."

"Twenty mil," Mr. Ellis rhapsodized. "Just think of what we could—"

"Sssh." Marilee leaned toward the TV. "I'm listening."

Her father gave her a look. "I thought you just said I had a better chance of—"

"Sssh!" she hissed again, leaning toward the TV. It was weird. She felt compelled to listen. And she was having the oddest sensations.

Physical, almost. Like her skin was electrified.

No. That was crazy. She shook off the feeling.

"But first," Timber Lee went on, "some southern Louisianans had themselves a good old time with Lotto fever today, as our reporter Rock Rockingham reports."

Marilee watched, dumbfounded, as videotape rolled of Weird Willie's impromptu Lotto Suckers event in Monument Square. There were hundreds of people gathered there, and in the center of them all was Weird Willie himself, on stilts, towering over the crowd, dressed in an Uncle Sam outfit.

"My man!" Marilee's father crowed with delight.

"Yo, suckers, this is what your Lotto tickets are worth!" Weird Willie yelled, about to torch a barrel full of dollar bills, which seemed to have been contributed by the people at the event.

"What a pig," Marilee fumed. "And what a waste."

"Aw, honey, don't take it so serious," her dad told her. "Weird Willie's just goofing on the whole thing."

"But think of how all that money could change someone's life. Maybe even—"

"Time for the drawing," Mr. Ellis interrupted.

Timber Lee was back on the TV. "Now let's go to Baton Rouge, for the Louisiana Lotto drawing."

Mr. Ellis closed his eyes. "Come on, baby," he murmured, rubbing his hands over his tickets for good luck.

On TV, the little Ping-Pong balls with Lotto numbers on them began to roll out of the Lotto machine, as a gorgeous spokesmodel called out the numbers.

Six. Sixteen. Twenty-one. Thirty-seven. Thirty-nine. Forty.

"And there you have it," Timber announced as her face filled the screen again. "Lucky Louisianan, who are you? Match those numbers to your lucky ticket, and come claim your prize. And if you come to the studios of Eyewitness News to do it, the champagne will be on us."

Mr. Ellis looked down at his Lotto tickets. Then he slowly tore them into tiny pieces and dropped them on the floor like the worthless confetti they had become.

Wordlessly, Marilee got up and went back to her room, closing the door behind her. She looked out the window at the full-mooned Louisiana sky.

A moonbeam fell on the Loverock, and the light caught her eye.

What good is a Loverock when the boy you love doesn't love you back? Marilee thought sadly. *What good is—*

Suddenly she gasped as if she had been punched in the stomach.

Propped up against the Loverock, exactly where she'd put it when she'd come home from Hava Java, was the Lotto ticket Marley had given her.

The numbers on it were barely visible in the moonlight.

But as Marilee read them, from left to right, it was as if each of them was aflame.

Six.

Sixteen.

Twenty-one.

Thirty-seven.

Thirty-nine.

And the last number was—

Oh my gosh.

Forty.

Chapter

8

All members of the Substance Z Recovery and
Field Test Team (SZR/FTT): identification of
field-test subject number two (Subject Two)
had been achieved. Name: Marilee Ellis. Age:
15. Residence: Overton, Louisiana.

Ms. Ellis is now to be referred to as Subject Two.

Subject Two was identified after she won the Louisiana Lotto jackpot. A photograph taken of Subject Two, her father, and her grandmother, in front of the mobile home where Subject Two and her father lived, was published in the New Orleans *Times-Picayune*.

In said photograph, Subject Two holds a check for twenty million dollars. She also holds an object that she calls the Loverock. Our computer analysis of photo confirms the Loverock to be a chunk of Substance Z. This appears to be the same chunk of Substance Z once in the possession of Subject One, Callie Bailey. Confirmation is pending.

Times-Picayune story accompanying the photo relates Subject Two "received the Loverock as a gift from her grandmother" the night before she was "given" her winning lottery ticket. (Note: Subject Two claims she did not purchase ticket herself, but will not say who gave it to her.)

Subject Two's grandmother claims she found Loverock in rear of her pickup truck after returning home from shopping. Thus far FTT has been unable to verify any other source. Possibility that grandmother might be part of foreign national organization seeking to steal Substance Z technology cannot be excluded. Further investigation is fast-tracked at this time.

Since winning Lotto, Subject Two and her father have moved into penthouse suite at Overton Inn and Hotel. Also in residence with some frequency is Subject Two's best friend, Karly Renwick, 15, of Carter, Louisiana. Renwick is home-schooled, so there is no truancy issue. Note Renwick lives in same town as Subject Two's grandmother. Investigation into Renwick's possible espionage involvement, and also any effect of Substance Z on Renwick, is ongoing.

Subject Two now being tailed by FTT to monitor effects of Substance Z and Mirror Image Effect (MIE). Question: was her winning the Louisiana Lotto a result of MIE? Because of Subject Two's high media profile, FTT must use all necessary secrecy to avoid compromising the operation.

Note: both Subject One (Callie Bailey of St. Charles Parish) and Subject Two are 15-year-old females. No other member of either subject's immediate family has exhibited MIE.

Might MIE work only on female subjects, age 15? Further study essential and ongoing.

On a different front: SZR/FTT successfully recovered four additional chunks of highly active Sub Z from two locales in Mississippi and two in west Texas. FTT notes that all four chunks of Sub Z assumed same heart shape as chunk in possession of Subject Two. Reason unknown at this time.

Computer simulations of return to earth and explosion of Subbie satellite indicate that at least fifty chunks of active Sub Z remain unaccounted for. It is essential that we recover all unaccounted for Sub Z and engage in covert surveillance of subjects who recover any stray chunks.

PROCEED WITH ALL DUE CAUTION. SHRED THIS DOCUMENT.

Chapter

9

Marilee was having the most incredible dream. She had won the Louisiana Lotto. She was richer than Olivia Fairmont, and she had become famous. She lived in a luxurious hotel penthouse, had a fantastic wardrobe, and everyone wanted to be friends with her. Even Livy. Olivia.

The best part of it all was, Adam was madly in love with her. They were in a very expensive, romantic restaurant and she was wearing a long gown that sparkled as she danced in Adam's arms. He looked into her eyes and told her how beautiful she looked. He confessed that he was in love with her. Then he tipped her chin up to him and gave her the most wonderful, fantastic kiss.

From behind, Marilee heard someone cry out. She turned around. There was Livy. She had seen Adam kissing Marilee and she was heart-broken. Black mascara mixed with the tears that tracked down her cheeks.

Really. Livy had turned out to be such a sore loser.

Marilee turned back to Adam.

Now, where were we? Ah, yes. She wrapped her arms around his neck, he put his arms around her slender waist, and—

Marilee woke up. Her eyes popped open.

No ball gown. No Adam with his arms around her.

But she laughed out loud anyway. And why shouldn't she? So much of what she had dreamed *was* true. She had won twenty million dollars a week before. She was living in the pent-house of what was the most exclusive hotel in Overton, and she wasn't at all worried about how she would pay the bill.

She was very, very rich.

"Good morning, New Orleans!" Weird Willie yelled maniacally from the living room radio. "It's a sizzling Saturday on the bayou, with temps expected to reach record-breaking highs today. So all you suckers who work in the great out-doors instead of in a refrigerated box like the one I'm in, break out that high-test deodorant, okay?"

"Ha!" Marilee heard her father bark at the radio.

Almost everything in her life had changed. But her father's delight in Weird Willie hadn't.

"Time for 'Tales of the Weird,' " Weird Willie went on. "Today we're talking with people who believe that our government is doing all kinds of top-secret covert stuff. I call 'em the *X-Files* loonies, and a few of the loonies are in the studio with me today. Hey, you loonies, maybe you oughta call up the Twenty Million Dollar Cinderella and see if she'll throw you some bucks to help your paranoid loony cause, huh?"

"Weird Willie's talkin' about you again, honey!" her father crowed from the suite's living room. "Did ya hear him, Marilee?"

"I heard. Now, please turn it down, Daddy!" Marilee called back.

Her father turned down the radio.

Marilee smiled and stretched. Imagine, Weird Willie talking about her on the radio. In fact, he'd talked about her every day since she'd won the Lotto.

But then, everyone was talking about her. "The Twenty Million Dollar Cinderella," the New Orleans *Times-Picayune* had dubbed her. Overnight, it seemed as if the whole nation had been taken by the story of the selfless single father and his beautiful, motherless teenage daughter.

They had struggled for so long to make ends meet, the stories all went, but now all their struggles were over.

It was all so overwhelming. Marilee had done so many interviews, and had been so busy, that her father had allowed her to stay out of school the entire week since she'd won the lottery. Thank goodness Karly's parents had allowed her to stay with Marilee for a while. Otherwise Marilee thought she would have freaked out completely.

Now Marilee padded from the lavish bathroom into Karly's room, towel-drying her hair. "I could get used to living like this," Karly said to her.

"It's so much more fun with you here," Marilee replied. "Ask your parents if you can move in with me permanently."

"Yeah, right," Karly scoffed. "I may have nice parents, and they may have said I could stay with you for a couple of weeks and bathe in your reflected glory—as long as I did my homework—but the day the fire chief of Carter lets his daughter live elsewhere permanently is the day—"

"He gets abducted by aliens!" the girls said together, laughing at Marilee's old excuse for everything.

The joke was funny, but the possibility of Marilee being abducted and held for ransom was not. So many people were after Marilee that her father was concerned about her well-being. He didn't want Marilee to return to school until he could hire a chauffeur and bodyguard for her. He'd finally decided on someone he already knew and trusted, his childhood friend Joey Souffet. When he wasn't with Marilee, Joey was staying in their trailer, taking care of Marilee's animals until she could find them all homes.

Everyone wanted to talk to Marilee. Bags of mail arrived at the hotel every day. People tried to meet her in the lobby, to speak to her, to touch her or that good-luck charm of a rock as if her good luck could somehow rub off on them.

Most of all, everyone wanted money from her.

Marilee didn't mind the attention, though. She felt like a rock star or a supermodel. In fact, she relished the idea of going back to school on Monday, to see how Olivia and Bree and their whole snobby clique would ooh and aah over her as she got out of her chauffeur-driven car.

It was going to be fun.

Now she sighed. "You know, if only Adam would pick up the stupid phone and call me, everything would be perfect," she told Karly.

"Call him," Karly said. "Or does the Twenty Million Dollar Princess hire someone to make her phone calls for her?"

Marilee hurled a pillow at Karly, which started a world-class pillow fight that didn't end until both girls were laughing so hard they had to stop to catch their breath.

Then, Karly threw on some clothes and went down to the lobby. She wanted to pick out cards at the gift shop to send to her friends in Carter, and run some errands. Marilee got back onto the luxurious bed, and thought back on the moment she realized that she really, truly had just won the Lotto.

She had first told her father, who'd almost fainted. Then she'd called Grammy, then Karly, and then, without hesitating for a moment, Adam. He hadn't been home, so she left a message on his machine.

He never called back.

When she and her dad moved to the Overton Inn, she'd called him again and given him the secret code word to use with the front desk of the hotel so they'd put his call through. He hadn't returned that call, either.

Today is the day he's going to call, Marilee told herself as she lay back down on her queen-size bed. *I just know it. He knows what happened. He's giving me time to recover. He's seen me on TV. Maybe he even saw the local news piece on that New Orleans beauty salon that gave me a free makeover, even though I could have paid them whatever they asked for. I look every bit as good as Olivia Fairmont now. Maybe better.*

Marilee looked around her huge, gorgeous

bedroom—the carpeting was rose-colored, so thick her feet got lost in it. The walls were pale pink, the ceiling twenty feet high. On the marble nightstand next to her bed was her own phone— pale pink to match the silk comforter on the bed.

She had her own big-screen TV and state-of-the-art CD player. A new Compaq computer. Three cameras that made the Nikon she used to borrow from school look like a toy. And a closet full of gorgeous clothes.

She padded over to the full-length mirror to gaze at her new, improved reflection. Last week, her hair had been trimmed and styled, with various subtle tones of blond streaked into it, just like Gwyneth Paltrow's, courtesy of the New Orleans salon. A famous makeup artist had taught Marilee how to do her makeup and a fashion consultant had helped her select her new wardrobe.

Every time she liked something, she bought it. French perfume? Bought it. Expensive makeup? Bought it. Designer clothes? Silk lingerie? Fabulous shoes? Bought it, bought it, bought it.

Marilee lifted her now much blonder hair off her neck and studied the effect in the mirror. Hmmm. That really did show off her new diamond studs nicely.

I could try to put it up myself, but why bother when I can just hire someone to do it?

She wandered over to the picture window

that looked down on the center of Overton. She could see Hava Java, where she no longer worked. And Zazu, the expensive boutique where she'd never been able to afford anything and the salesgirl Roxie had been so mean to her.

Two days before, just like in the movies, Marilee and Karly had gone into Zazu and told the manager that if only that salesgirl Roxie hadn't been so mean to Marilee back when Marilee was poor, Marilee would now be spending a small fortune in Zazu.

"You really need to train your help to be more welcoming," Marilee had suggested.

"Because you never know when a nobody is going to be a somebody," Karly had added.

"In fact," Marilee had added, "you never know when someone you think *is* a nobody is a somebody."

It had been one of the more satisfying moments of Marilee's life.

Afterward Karly and she had gone to the Overton ASPCA animal shelter and paid the adoption fees for anyone who wanted to adopt out an animal during an entire month.

That had been incredibly satisfying, too.

Now, Marilee leaned close to the window and frowned. That big, black sedan was parked on a side street again, just around the corner from Overton Naturals. She'd seen it three times in the past week. Once she'd actually walked past it and noticed that the windows were tinted so dark she couldn't see inside.

The car gave her a creepy feeling. But she shrugged it off.

She had no way of knowing she was being watched carefully by the Substance Z surveillance team.

"Hey, Marilee!" her dad called from the living room.

She went inside to join him.

"What do you think of your old man now?" Her father was wearing a designer shirt and pants, and sunglasses. He turned in a circle, modeling for her.

"You look like someone famous."

"Hey, I *am* someone famous. I'm the proud pop of the Twenty Million Dollar Cinderella." He took off the sunglasses. "I got a dozen pairs of these glasses and a dozen of these Irish linen shirts. In assorted colors that compliment my skin tones, which is the way you're supposed to do it, according to my personal shopper."

"Of course," Marilee agreed with mock seriousness.

Her father let out a whoop of delight. "I keep thinking someone is gonna pinch me and I'm gonna wake up and it's all gonna be a dream."

"I know the feeling, Daddy."

Marilee excused herself, took a quick shower, put on another of her many expensive new outfits, and was drying her hair when her dad knocked on the door to tell that her breakfast had arrived.

The tuxedoed waiter was just finishing setting up breakfast on a snowy white tablecloth on the dining room table. He'd brought a vase of red roses for a centerpiece.

Her father signed for the check with a flourish, adding a generous tip. The waiter practically bowed his way out of the room, he was so happy.

"I ordered that kiwi fruit you like. Double order. Strawberries with fresh whipped cream. And chocolate chip pancakes," her dad reported. "Good thing you inherited your old man's fast metabolism, huh? We both stay thin no matter how much we eat."

"Was my mother thin?" Marilee asked softly as she poured syrup on her pancakes. "You always say I look like her, right down to this." She pointed to the heart-shaped birthmark on her forearm. "So I just wondered."

Her father put the linen napkin to his lips and laughed nervously. "I believe that's the first time you ever asked a single thing about her, Marilee. I'm always the one who brings her up."

Marilee shrugged, looking around the opulent room. "I was just thinking how much she would have loved all this. Wouldn't she have?"

"Who wouldn't?" Her father's voice sounded funny. He took a sip of his juice. "Fresh-squeezed. Can't beat it. So, what's up for you today?"

"Remember, I told you I'm doing that ribbon-cutting downtown for the New Orleans Tourism Bureau?"

Her father pretended to frown. "They paying you?"

"Daddy!" She laughed.

The mayor of New Orleans himself had called Marilee, to ask if the Twenty Million Dollar Cinderella would join him at a ceremonial ribbon-cutting for the new tourism information center on Bourbon Street in the French Quarter. He said the city would make a generous donation to Marilee's favorite charity as compensation.

Marilee had readily agreed and asked that the money be donated to the ASPCA.

"So my little girl's a spokesmodel, too," her dad said, beaming. "I always told you you were beautiful, didn't I? Listen, Joey's driving you to this thing, Marilee. Be sure to call and tell him what time."

"I will. Karly's coming, too."

Her father poured himself more coffee. "Hey, Grammy called. She said if you'd go to church with her tomorrow, she'd let you buy her a fancy outfit. But I practically had to twist her arm to agree to the last part."

"I wish she'd move in with us, Daddy."

"I'd get down on my knees if I thought it

would budge the woman. But you know Grammy. She won't leave Carter and the friends she loves. Me, I say good riddance to bad rubbish."

"I love Carter," Marilee said. "It's not rubbish."

Her father snorted his opinion. "You just don't know how it really is, Marilee. Without the factory, that town is dead, and the folks still there are just too stupid to give it a funeral and wave *adios.*"

But they care about each other, Marilee thought as she sipped her coffee. *It would be like breaking up your family just because someone in it got really sick.*

"Oh, listen, sweetie, I meant to tell you," her father went on. "What with all the phone calls and letters from everybody with a sob story wanting us to write 'em a big fat check, I hired a secretary to screen all that stuff for us. She starts Monday."

"That's a good idea."

"She'll be here while you're at school." Her father sipped his coffee. "It's amazing how many people want a handout."

Marilee sipped her coffee and frowned. "But some of the letters are heartbreaking, Dad," she told him. "Little kids who need operations that their parents can't afford. People whose homes burned down. Farmers who lost—"

"So what're you gonna do, tell 'em to form a

line and start writing checks? Once you start, Marilee, where do you stop?"

At that moment the phone rang.

Mr. Ellis threw his hands in the air. "See what I mean? What kind of help is this hotel hiring?"

"I'll get it." Marilee practically flew across the room to the phone.

Please let it be Adam, she prayed. *Please, please, please, please let it be—*

She snatched up the phone. "Hello?"

"Hello, may I speak to Marilee?"

The voice was female. Marilee sat, very disappointed. "Who's calling?" she asked warily.

"This is Logan Calhoun. I'm a friend of Marilee's."

Now, this is a surprise, Marilee thought. *She must not recognize my voice. She must think I'm the housekeeper. Or something. Ah, the first of the superficial Livy squad to decide I'm okay enough for them to be friends with me. One down, two to go.*

"Miss Ellis isn't in right now," Marilee said smoothly.

"May I leave a message for her then?"

"You may."

"Please tell her that Adam Eagleton gave me her number, and the code name to give the hotel operator so that my call could go through. He said he was sure Marilee wouldn't mind. Oh, and could you tell her I'm staying in Overton longer than I thought, and I'd really like her to call me. She has the number at the Calhouns'."

"Um-hmm," Marilee murmured, feigning utter boredom.

"Did you need me to repeat my name? It's—"

"No. Thank you. Good-bye." Marilee hung up.

"Who was that, another loser looking for a freebie?" her father asked.

Marilee laughed. "That was the sound of the worm turning, Daddy. The worm turning."

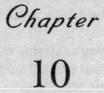

$\mathcal{M}$arilee checked her reflection in her full-length mirror one last time. Darling designer dress. Strappy new sandals. Perfect hair and makeup.

"Yes, the Twenty Million Dollar Cinderella is ready for her photo opportunity," she told her reflection.

"So young, so rich, and yet so obnox—I mean humble," Karly teased.

Marilee laughed and plopped down on her bed next to Karly. "I still feel like none of this is real."

"Maybe it isn't. Maybe we're both stuck in the same dream. That'd be kinda cool, huh?"

"You read too much science fiction," Marilee told her.

"Hey, my parents are happy I read anything. You know how they are—no TV until all your work is done, why don't you read a book instead, blah-blah-blah."

"Well, while you're staying with me, you can watch TV until your eyes fall out. Especially since I'm about to be on it."

"Again," Karly added.

Marilee shrugged. "It's fun. Some of the time, anyway. And this time it's to raise money for the ASPCA."

"How about if we just adopt all the animals there instead?"

Marilee laughed. "Can you imagine them running around this hotel? The concierge would have a heart attack." She sighed. "I miss my animals. Especially Dog the cat."

Karly's eyes twinkled. "Let's sneak Dog up here. And after that, we can go to Carter and wait for the alarms to go off at the firehouse. There's nothing like a towering inferno to make a girl's day."

Marilee laughed. "You are a very strange person."

"Thank you," Karly said. "I'd better jump in the shower and get reasonably cute before Joey comes to pick us up, even if I'm not the one who's going to be on TV."

Karly disappeared into the bathroom, and Marilee glanced at the clock.

I've got twenty minutes before Joey comes to pick me up and take us to Bourbon Street for the ribbon-cutting, Marilee thought as she reached for the remote control and flipped the TV on. She ran through the channels, but there was nothing on she wanted to watch.

She felt restless. Her eyes kept being drawn to the three bulging canvas bags of mail that sat against the wall of her room. All of them were filled with letters she'd received from strangers.

Daddy may think it's stupid, she thought, *but I want to read some of that mail before his secretary sends each of them a form letter or a postcard or something.*

She crouched in front of the mailbags. Somehow, she was drawn to the canvas bag on the far left. She untied its roughly drawn knot and thrust her hand inside, digging, digging, digging.

All the way to the bottom of the sack.

She grabbed a fistful of mail.

No. None of them was right. Whatever *that* meant. She had the weirdest feeling that there was a single letter in that bag that she *must* read.

Something important.

She reached into the bag again, rooting around crazily at the bottom. When her fingers closed around a certain envelope, she felt them tingle. But that was nuts—she knew she had to be imagining it.

The feeling was really strong, though. So she

plucked the envelope out and took the letter over to her bed, and then had the sense that the letter was actually *buzzing* in her fingers.

Weird.

The white envelope was neatly addressed. There was no return address. All that was in the upper left-hand corner of the envelope was the name CALLIE.

Marilee tore it open and read.

Dear Marilee,

My name is Callie, and before you throw this letter out, I am NOT ASKING FOR MONEY OR FOR ANYTHING. The reason I'm writing is much more important. I saw your photo in the newspaper where you're holding the Loverock. What I am about to tell you is going to sound really bizarre, but I swear it is the total truth. I had a Loverock, too, exactly like yours. I found it the morning after that big meteor exploded over New Orleans. I read in the newspaper that you said that once you got the Loverock, your life totally changed. The exact same thing happened to me. That's why we must meet ASAP. I feel we are connected somehow. Everything inside of me is telling me that this is extremely urgent. Please call me. THIS IS NOT A PRANK AND I AM NOT A LUNATIC. My phone number is 555-6854.

—Callie

Marilee was glad Karly was in the bathroom. Otherwise, she was sure her friend would have heard her heart beating double-time. Her breathing grew shallow and rapid. She felt the letter growing hot in her hands, until she had to drop it on the bed like a burning ember.

THIS IS NOT A PRANK AND I AM NOT A LUNATIC.

"Well, if you were a lunatic you wouldn't very well say you were one in the letter," Marilee muttered aloud.

And yet, something inside of her was telling her that this girl Callie—whoever she was—wasn't crazy. Carefully, she picked up the letter again. Instantly, she felt electric surges running from the letter into her fingers.

"Okay, this is really out there," Marilee said.

Pick up the phone. Call her. Call her now, a voice inside Marilee's head said.

That made her drop the letter again. Because the voice had been hers. But the *thought* had come from someplace deep inside of her that Marilee hadn't even known existed, some higher place of knowing, acutely in tune with—

This was getting entirely too bizarre, like something out of one of those science-fiction novels Karly loved to read.

Marilee could just hear her dad saying, *She's a scam artist, sweetie. She knows you're getting a million letters asking for money, so she sends you some psychic mumbo-jumbo to get you to call her, and then she'll hit you up for the bucks. It's a new angle on an old game, Marilee.*

Marilee scanned the letter.

I feel we are connected somehow.

Truth, said that voice deep inside of her.

Lie, she told herself.

She forced herself to put the letter aside, went back to the mailbag, and took out six more, which she read quickly. Four of them asked for money. One said that aliens were coming to abduct Marilee; since that was her old excuse for running late all the time, it made her laugh.

The sixth said that the letter-writer and she were long-lost identical twins and claimed they were the secret love children of Harrison Ford.

Which is just about as likely as my big "connection" to Callie-who-isn't-a-lunatic, Marilee thought. *Dad is right. These are all scam artists or loonies.*

Karly came out of the bathroom, freshly showered, dressed in cute overalls and a T-shirt. "Your bathroom is so nice I could live in there," she announced. "I wonder what—"

She stopped as she took in Marilee's pale face.

I feel we are connected somehow.

"Marilee?" Karly asked. "You okay?"

"Fine," Marilee told her. "I'm fine."

Karly didn't look convinced.

"Really, I'm fine," Marilee insisted. "Hey, let's both wear that new perfume I bought. We'll be irresistible."

As they spritzed each other with the perfume, Marilee kept being drawn back to the letter on the bed in the plain white envelope, the one without a return address.

"And now, to cut the ribbon and open the city of New Orleans's new Bourbon Street Tourist Information Center, it's my pleasure to introduce Louisiana's very own Twenty Million Dollar Cinderella, Miss Marilee Ellis!" the mayor announced.

The crowd of about two hundred people applauded as Marilee gave Karly's hand a little squeeze before stepping forward. She took a giant pair of scissors from the mayor and snipped the pink ribbon that draped across the double glass doors to the tourist bureau. As she did, photographers clicked her photo, and a Dixieland band began wailing out "When the Saints Come Marching In."

The crowd then surged forward, eager to get to the free refreshments and gift giveaways inside the new office. Fortunately Joey Souffet was a large man who took his job as bodyguard seriously. He edged against Marilee, his eyes hyperalert for any potential threat to her.

What he couldn't protect her from were the

telephoto lenses of the Substance Z reconnaissance team, covertly videotaping the whole event from an office building across the street.

Marilee hurried back over to her friend.

"Your ribbon-cutting skills are legendary," Karly told Marilee. "This could be a career path."

"Marilee, Marilee, over here!" people began to shout.

"Uh, this is where I make my graceful exit," Karly said. "I'll meet you back at the car."

Marilee gave her friend a thumbs-up before being besieged by people.

"Marilee! Marilee!"

"Marilee! Hey, want to marry me?"

"I got this great business idea, Marilee—"

Everyone was yelling, trying to talk to her as Joey hovered protectively.

"I just want your autograph!" a girl cried, thrusting a piece of paper at Marilee. Marilee signed autograph after autograph, feeling a little ridiculous.

It's not like I'm famous for having accomplished something, she thought.

The crowd pressed in, and Joey put his arm protectively around Marilee's shoulder. "I think it's time to get out of here," he said. Shielding her with his body, he led her toward the car.

A skinny old woman leaped forward, her eyes

bulging into Marilee's face. "Thief!" she shouted. "Thief! You stole my money!"

Marilee shrank back, horrified, as Joey positioned himself between her and the old woman.

"Marilee! Marilee! It's me! Callie!" a girl's voice cut through the din.

Callie? The Callie?

Marilee's eyes scanned the crowd, searching.

"Better get in the car," Joey advised, holding the door open for her. "This situation ain't safe."

"Marilee! Marilee! It's me! Callie!"

"I want to talk to Callie," Marilee said, craning her neck, looking for the source of the voice.

"Who's Callie?" Joey asked, bewildered.

"I don't know," Marilee said honestly. "But—"

And then, there she was. Standing in front of her.

Callie.

She was beautiful in an original way. Dark hair, geeky-cool retro-50s glasses, black jeans and a T-shirt.

"Did you get my letter?" Callie asked breathlessly.

Marilee nodded, her eyes locked with the girl's. She couldn't look away. Her body felt almost shimmery.

"You know what I said is the truth," Callie realized. "I see it in your eyes. Listen, we have to talk—"

"Did you get *my* letter, Marilee?" someone else cried.

"How about my letter? On purple paper!"

"Repent, Marilee! Repent for stealing my money!"

"Hey, Marilee, let's book, this is creepy," Karly called, sticking her head out the window of the car.

The crowd pushed in.

"But—" Marilee objected.

Joey gently but firmly edged Marilee into the car, where Karly grabbed her hand protectively.

"I'll call you!" Marilee yelled to Callie, just before Joey climbed in and put up the automatic windows. "I will!"

"Whoa, major scene, huh?" Karly said. "Who's that girl?"

"I'll explain when we get back to the hotel. You won't believe this."

As soon as they got back, Marilee ran to her room to get Callie's letter from her bed.

Only there was nothing there.

Her dad had decided to bring in their new secretary early so she could start to send preprinted postcards to everyone. She had picked up all the mail that had been in Marilee's room, including what had been on her bed.

Except for the mail that had no return addresses on it. Those letters and cards had been thrown into the hotel Dumpster.

And burned.

They included a certain white envelope that had been marked only CALLIE.

Marilee told Karly all about the letter she had gotten from Callie, and how Callie supposedly had a Loverock of her own.

But without the actual letter, the story sounded incredibly lame.

"Looks like one of your fans followed you to school," Joey said as he pulled the car up to the front of Overton High on Monday morning. Kids were streaming into school, but some of them stopped to gawk at Marilee's car. In the midst of all the kids was a pale older lady holding a crudely lettered sign:

MARILEE CINDERELLA
I MUST TALK TO YOU

Marilee didn't want to think about the woman right then. She had been waiting for this day for a long time—her triumphant return to Overton High. The day Olivia and Bree and their mean, snotty friends would all be in awe of the new Marilee.

"That's sad, huh?" Joey said, peering at the woman.

"It's all just so . . . so depressing. I mean, when does the parade stop?"

Joey peered at her. "You're starting to sound just like your old man. There's a lot of neediness in the world, Marilee."

"I know that. But there are a lot of people who just want to mooch off other people, too. Everyone wants a handout." Marilee looked around for Olivia and her friends. She didn't want to get out of the car until she was sure they were watching.

"We got a saying back in Carter," Joey said dryly. " 'You can't judge a book by its cover.' "

Marilee didn't respond. She was too busy wondering where Olivia was. Livy and Bree always walked into school at the last possible moment, so everyone could admire whatever cool new outfits they'd chosen to wear.

Joey grunted. "You know what I remember?"

Marilee sighed. "What?"

"Who your dad used to be. Back home, before the factory closed, and especially before you won all this money. He was the kinda person who cared about what's really important. Like your Grammy."

"Um-hmmm," Marilee murmured, not really listening. She couldn't *believe* Olivia had already gone into school.

Joey could see Marilee wasn't paying any attention to him, so he ended his lecture. "I'll watch you until you get into the building. And I'll fetch you right here after school. Don't be late. Any problems, you push that panic beeper I gave you, all right?"

He got out and held the door for Marilee, who regally stepped out of the car.

Instantly, she was recognized. For a few moments it was bedlam as kids crowded around to congratulate her on winning the lottery. Then, all too quickly, it was over. The warning bell sounded to alert everyone that school would be starting in three minutes.

Marilee headed inside.

Logan Calhoun came up beside her. "Marilee, hi, congratulations!"

What is Logan Calhoun doing at Overton High?

Marilee eyed her coolly as they walked down the hall together. She saw this as her first chance to turn the tables on those snobs.

"Oh. Hello."

"I stayed on with my aunt and uncle because of some family prob—well, it's complicated," Logan said. "Anyway, I'm going to go to school here for a while. It's horrible being the new girl, I have to tell you."

"Poor you," Marilee said coldly. "But I'm sure it's a comfort to have so many wonderful friends here already."

Logan gave her a strange look. "Did you get my message at the hotel?"

Marilee's eyes flicked over to her. "Did you call? Who did you leave it with? The *housekeeper?*"

"I think that's who it was."

Marilee shrugged. "I get zillions of messages. It must have gotten lost in the pile or something."

"Maybe," Logan said. "Well, see you, I guess."

She sounded hurt, and for a moment Marilee felt bad about it. But then she remembered that Logan was friends with Livy. So she just walked away, thinking that it was so much more satisfying to be the one doing the dissing instead of being the one getting dissed.

Marilee turned the corner.

And there were Olivia and Bree, standing right outside her homeroom.

Ah, the moment I've been waiting for. Watching them suck up like Logan just did is going to be the best, Marilee thought. *Mirror, mirror on the wall, the poor girl is now the richest of them all. So how do you like that, Olivia Fairmont?*

Olivia spotted her. "Oh, look, it's Cinderella!"

"Marilee Cinderella, hi!" Bree cried.

Marilee flicked her hair off her face with a practiced shake of her head and sauntered over to them. "Oh, hi," she said laconically. "Cute outfit, Livy."

Olivia's eyes lit up. "You really think so? Really?" She turned to Bree. "She likes my outfit!"

"Oh, that's so *fantastic!* How about my outfit?" Bree asked nervously.

"Darling," Marilee decreed.

"Oh, thanks," Bree gushed. "Really, thanks!"

"It's nothing," Marilee murmured.

Olivia turned to Marilee. "I have a riddle for you. Want to hear it?"

"Okay," Marilee said.

"What do you call trash who suddenly gets rich?" Olivia asked.

"I dunno," Bree cut in. "What *do* you call trash who suddenly gets rich?"

Olivia chortled, "The answer is: Trash!"

Olivia and Bree cracked up.

Marilee froze.

"What's the matter, Cinderella?" Olivia jeered. "Did you really think that just because someone gave you the magic slipper you'd stop being trash?"

Marilee's mouth opened, but no sound came out. She was mute in the presence of Olivia's power.

"You're trash, Marilee," Olivia went on. "Your father is trash, your mother *was* trash, and all *you'll ever be* is trash. Because you know what they say. You can dress it up, but you can never wash away the stench."

She sniffed the air, then she and Bree held their noses ostentatiously.

Then, laughing together, they strode away in triumph.

Marilee stood there, rooted to the spot.

They had reduced her to someone ridiculous and pathetic.

Maybe I am ridiculous, Marilee thought, gulping down a lump in her throat. *They can say whatever they want to say about me. But they're wrong about something else.*

Marilee brushed a tear from her eye. "Y'all are wrong," she whispered fiercely after them. "My mother was not trash."

Chapter

11

$\mathcal{M}$arilee read the note from Adam for maybe the hundredth time.

When she'd come back to the hotel after school the day before, the concierge had handed her everything in her coded mailbox.

There was a note from Ms. Pfeffer, asking Marilee when she'd have her entry for the Y.A.A. ready.

And there was a note from Adam.

Marilee—
You won't see me at school today because this is the day when everyone in the mentor program gets to go to work with their mentor. I'll be in a recording studio in New Orleans, watching Mon-

roe LaCrue lay down tracks for his new CD. So, anyway, I know we haven't talked. But I hate the phone and we can't really talk at school. My parents want to know if you would take some nature photos they can blow up and put on the walls at Overton Naturals. Not that you need money, but they don't expect you to do it for free. We could go get the shots tomorrow morning since it's an in-service day. Maybe it would give us a chance to talk, too. So call me if you want.

—*Adam*

She'd gone upstairs immediately and called, but got his machine again.

This time, though, he called her back.

The conversation was a little weird. Stilted. Like two people who didn't really know each other.

Still, they made arrangements to meet in the hotel lobby at eight the next morning.

Marilee barely slept because she'd been so excited. She called Karly immediately after she had gotten off the phone with Adam. They had analyzed the entire conversation. Karly's sage advice had been "Be yourself."

Whatever that means, Marilee thought nervously as she checked herself out in the mirror.

She'd gotten up extra early to have plenty of time to dress and do her makeup. Now, she was ready—and she was really early. So she sat on her bed and quickly dialed Karly's number.

"Karly here, where's the fire?" Karly answered as always.

"In my stomach," Marilee replied. "I'm all ready to go meet Adam, but I feel like the Dixie Chicks are throwing a party in my intestines."

"It's *Adam*," Karly reminded her.

"But everything is different now."

"Why, cuz you're rich? Get over it."

"Oh, thanks, that's *so* helpful," Marilee moaned.

"It's just money, Marilee. It's not like it's something important."

"Yeah, well, I've tried poor and I've tried rich," Marilee said. "And after completing this highly scientific study, I can tell you rich is better."

"You sure?"

"Of course, I'm sure."

"Well, I just meant that you and Adam had a much better relationship before you won the—"

"I didn't change, *he* did."

"You sure?"

"Stop saying that!" Marilee exclaimed.

"Oh, sorry. I thought you were asking my opinion."

Marilee sighed. "I did. Sorry. Pretend I'm on fire and come spray me down with 7-Up. It's what I deserve."

"You're just nervous because the guy of your dreams is on his way over and you could still blow the whole thing."

"That doesn't exactly help," Marilee said.

"Okay, how about this? When you look at Adam, picture him pre-hunk. It never made you nervous to be around him in the good ol' days."

"Hmmm. That's a good idea. I'll try," Marilee promised. "Thanks."

"No prob," Karly said easily. "Well, I'm off to spend the day showing little kids how a fire truck works. It's to raise money for the Retired Fire-fighters Relief Fund. It'd be more fun if I was actually part of the department, but whatever."

"Have fun."

"I will. Dave'll be there."

"Dave?"

"This guy who just moved in across the street. So cute."

Marilee laughed. "What happened to—whoever the last one was?"

"I'm in my flighty stage," Karly said blithely. "Hey, Marilee? I'm glad you're taking photos today."

Marilee was taken aback. "Why?"

"Because you love that as much as I love fire-fighting. And lately it seems like you've kinda given up what you love the most."

They said good-bye and Marilee hung up. She tucked Adam's letter into her backpack and went into the living room, where her father was drinking coffee and reading the newspaper.

"No Weird Willie this morning?" Marilee asked.

Her father was frowning. "I wanted to talk with you, sweetie. I know I said you could go out with Adam this morning without Joey coming along, but—"

"But what? I didn't win the Lotto so that I could live in a cage for the rest of my life—"

"Some cage," her father said dryly. "Look, all this attention will die down eventually. Maybe then—"

Marilee sat next to him and took his hands. "I waited so long for Adam to call me, Daddy. I can't wait until 'eventually' to spend time with him without Joey around."

Her father looked surprised. "You and Adam? But he's your buddy!"

He caught the look on her face.

"You're sweet on him," her dad declared.

She smiled shyly.

Her father pointed at her. "You just remember, little girl, I didn't kiss your mama until after we were engaged. She was a lady. And I expect you to be one, too."

"You don't have to worry about that, Daddy."

His frown grew. "Now I *really* don't think I should let you out without Joey—"

"I know you trust me. And I know you trust Adam."

Her father grumbled under his breath. "I have certain conditions. Joey drives you and Adam to the woods. You wear the panic beeper Joey gave

117

you. And you call me on your cell phone on the hour, every hour."

"Daddy—" Marilee protested.

"This is not negotiable." He folded his arms. "You're not going to be a kidnapping headline in the newspaper."

He feels protective because of losing Mama in that car accident, she realized.

Marilee leaned over and kissed his cheek. "Fine, Daddy. I will."

He gave her a hug. "That's my girl."

Marilee had no way of knowing that the whole conversation was being recorded by a tiny bug that had been planted in the chandelier. It had been easy for one of the Substance Z surveillance team members to impersonate a hotel employee, gain access to the suite, and plant the bug when no one was home.

Now, outside the hotel, in a nondescript-looking panel truck parked across the street, the team listened to every word.

The only sounds were of branches and leaves crunching beneath their shoes as Marilee and Adam tramped through the woods. Every once in a while Marilee would stop and take a picture. And even though she felt ridiculous doing it, she had dutifully called her father at nine o'clock.

"I'm here. Adam's here. I'm fine. Bye."

And that had been the extent of the excitement thus far. And of the conversation.

Climbing over a tree stump, Marilee stumbled, the stupid panic button she wore around her neck smacking her in the face.

"Didn't it occur to you that wearing that outfit into the woods would be kind of useless?" Adam asked.

"I'll have you know that Natalie Portman wore this exact outfit and these very same shoes in *Seventeen.*"

"Oh well, then, that certainly explains why you wore them *hiking.*"

She gave him a look, and he shrugged.

"Hey, look." Adam pointed up a tree to a man-made perch, reachable by a ten-foot ladder that had been nailed to the tree.

"Tree stand," Marilee said. Sometimes her father went hunting with his old buddies from Carter. They had always eaten everything he shot—deer, rabbits, whatever.

"You might get some great pictures from up there," Adam mused. "You up for it?" He eyed her expensive outfit and her clunky shoes warily.

"I could climb that ladder with one hand tied behind my back, Adam Eagleton, and still leave you in the dust."

For the first time, he grinned at her like he used to.

And for the first time, she grinned back.

"Race ya!" they both yelled, then took off toward the ladder. His work boots got him there much quicker than she got there. He scrambled up the ladder, then turned to give her a hand.

"No help necessary." Her shoe almost slid off the last rung and he caught her under the arms, lifting her onto the perch.

For just a moment his arms stayed around her. His face was so close to hers. She raised her lips.

There was a loud rustling in the woods.

"What was that?" She jumped away from him, alert, her hand on her panic button. "Do you think someone followed us?"

"It was a woodland creature, Marilee," Adam said dryly. "Cleverly named because it's a creature who lives in the woods."

"Ha-ha." She took her thumb off the panic button, feeling foolish. "You don't know what it's been like. People grab me. Everyone wants something. And then Daddy's so nervous all the time that someone is going to kidnap me that he has me—"

"Pushing the panic button over a chipmunk," Adam filled in as the little brown animal scampered by. "Good thing. Those little suckers can get homicidal."

Marilee laughed. Adam always could make her laugh.

"So, I guess your whole life has changed,"

Adam said, scratching his chin. He laughed self-consciously. "There's a big 'duh,' huh?"

"Daddy's new saying is, 'Rich or poor, it's nice to have money.' " She shook her head with wonder. "It still seems like a dream, you know? One day everything is horrible, and then Grammy gives me the Loverock, and then—"

"You don't really believe you won the lottery because Grammy gave you some *rock*, do you?"

"I know it sounds crazy, Adam, but I do. There's something magical about it."

He raised one doubtful eyebrow. "You been reading sci-fi with Karly?"

"I'm serious," Marilee insisted. "I got a letter from this girl named Callie. She had a Loverock, too, and it changed her life as much as it changed mine, and—"

"She *said* she had a Loverock, too. And you *believed* her?" Adam asked incredulously.

Marilee gave him a level gaze. "Because she was telling me the truth."

He was about to make another remark when something intense—burning, even—in Marilee's eyes stopped him. This was something he'd never seen before.

"Maybe she was," he found himself saying.

That Adam believed her made Marilee feel so close to him that she was bold enough to take his hand. She couldn't, however, look him in the eye.

Adam and I are holding hands!

"So, how was that mentor thing yesterday?" she asked, feigning utter nonchalance.

"Monroe is awesome. And the studio was amazing. He's letting me record the songs for Olivia in the sixteen-track studio during off-hours."

"Gee, that's nice," Marilee said, but she pulled her hand away.

"The Fairmonts aren't paying me for my studio time, Marilee. You know what that time actually costs? Or are you so rich now that you don't give a hoot about things like that anymore?"

Marilee turned to him. "And here I thought it was all about your *art,* not about money."

Adam stared at her. "Yeah, well, what about *your* art?"

"What about it?"

"What about your entry for Y.A.A.?"

"What's the point, really? The winners get to spend a summer at Rhode Island School of Design. So what? If I want to go to Rhode Island School of Design, I don't need to win a contest now to do it."

"No," Adam said slowly. "I guess you don't, Marilee, but you do have to be good enough to get in."

"I know that," she said, feeling a little irritated. She raised the camera and clicked off a shot of the sun through the leaves, just for something to do.

"So then you must really be working on your photography, huh? Like, how many hours a day are you spending on it? Just out of curiosity."

She looked at him.

Don't lie to him, she told herself, practically hearing Karly's voice in her head. *You've never lied to him.*

"Okay, zero," she said defensively. "But don't look at me like that. People work hard so they can make money. Well, I've got all the money I could ever spend in this lifetime, and then some. So why should I work?"

His face hardened. "If that's how you feel, why did you agree to take these photos, then?"

"I'm starting to wonder the same thing."

She turned as far away from him as the perch allowed, and pretended to get very busy taking photographs.

How can you not see how much I love you? her heart silently screamed. *I just held your hand! How can you still love Olivia and not love me, when she's such a horrid person?*

How can you?

A twig cracked. And another.

"Deer, Marilee," Adam whispered, his voice hoarse with excitement. "Over there. Three o'clock. No quick motions. Slow moves. I can see a doe. And a fawn. No, two fawns."

Marilee saw them, too. They were so beautiful. She quickly and quietly switched to a tele-photo lens, and raised the camera. The fawns were very young, with prominent white markings. They moved toward the tree stand, oblivious to the fact that two humans hung above them.

Silently, Marilee raised the camera and clicked off shot after shot. It was perfect—the dappled light through the trees, the graceful animals and their total lack of self-consciousness. Again and again she gently pushed the shutter release of her camera, capturing the magical moments.

The doe stopped feeding and cocked her head, standing completely still. Then she lifted her head higher and sniffed.

Human scent.

She bolted, her fawns running behind her on their spindly legs.

"Wow," Adam said. "You got that?"

Marilee tapped her camera. "Right here. Forever."

He gazed at her. "I wish you could see it."

Puzzled, she asked, "See what?"

"How your eyes are shining right now. So beautiful."

"They are?"

"More than any Loverock could ever shine, Marilee," Adam whispered, smoothing some hair off her face. "Not because you're rich. Or because you're wearing an outfit some actress wore in a magazine. Because you're doing what you love."

It's because I'm with the guy I love, she thought. *I have to tell him. Now.*

She gulped hard. There was something she had to know first.

Livy. How did he really feel about her?

"Adam," she said, her eyes searching his. "I want to ask you something and I have to know the truth. About L—"

A sound stopped her. Twigs cracked under the feet of what had to be a large animal.

"More deer?" she whispered.

Adam shook his head. "Too noisy." He wriggled his eyebrows at her. "Maybe a Marilee-eating bear!"

"Very funny." She didn't want to admit how nervous the sound was making her. "No one's seen bear around here in . . . well, forever."

"Just think how valuable a bear photo would be," Adam teased.

"Oh, you—"

Whatever it was, it was coming closer.

Up in their tree, they were absolutely still, waiting.

Marilee licked her lips nervously, tasting her own fear. *What if it's the most dangerous animal of all?* she thought. *A human. Humans. Who tracked us up here to kidnap me.*

She felt Adam reach for her hand.

Her heart was racing, her breath short. She touched the panic button.

Adam stopped her. He pointed. Their stalker had come into view.

Human.

A lone woman.

Middle-aged, pale, with grayish hair.

"Marilee?" the woman called into the woods. "Marilee Ellis? Where are you?"

"Hey, I recognize her," Marilee said to Adam. "She was hanging around school yesterday. With some sign."

"You want to go down and talk to her?" Adam asked. "She looks harmless enough."

"What she looks is sad. We'll have to listen to some long sob story about her terrible life and how poor she is, and then she'll ask for a handout."

"So what if she is poor." Adam touched Marilee's hand, so that she'd look at him. "You used to be poor, too, remember?"

He was right.

And it hadn't been so long ago, either, she thought.

"Hey! Hey! Up here!" Marilee called, making a quick decision.

The woman looked around, trying to locate the sound of Marilee's voice. So Marilee scrambled down the tree, Adam following her. They walked over to the woman.

"Marilee?" the woman rasped. "Is it really you?"

"It's me." Marilee's heart went out to the woman, whose face looked so sad and worn.

Marilee and her father had struggled, yes. But to be *this* poor? Poor enough to follow someone into the woods, to beg? It must be horrible.

"What's your name?" Marilee asked gently.

The woman didn't speak for a long moment. "You got a cigarette?" she finally asked.

"We don't smoke," Adam said. "I have some granola bars in my backpack, though. If you're hungry."

The woman fixed her eyes on him. "Aren't we the little patronizing one? Who are you, the good fairy?"

"That would be news to me," Adam replied, more bemused than offended.

"You her sweetheart?" the woman asked bluntly.

"That really isn't any of your business," Marilee replied quickly.

For some reason, this made the woman laugh.

Marilee folded her arms. "I saw you at my school yesterday, didn't I?"

"If you saw me, why didn't you talk to me?"

"I can't talk to everyone who wants to talk to me," Marilee explained. "It's dangerous."

"Do I look like everyone?" the woman demanded.

"You look like someone . . . who needs a friend," Marilee said, choosing her words carefully. She was beginning to think that this woman wasn't entirely stable.

"Oh, do I?" The woman asked in a mocking voice. "I had a lot of friends once. A family, too."

Marilee slowly took a step backward. Maybe this hadn't been such a good idea after all. She and Adam traded uncertain looks.

Suddenly all the bombast seemed to leave the woman. She sagged against the tree. "I'm sorry. I'm doing this all wrong."

Marilee forced herself to touch the woman's hand. "It's all right," she said softly. "What did you want to say to me?"

"I thought up close you'd recognize me," the woman said sadly. "Because we look so much alike."

Marilee shook her head. "What are you talking about?"

"Marilee, I'm your mother."

Suddenly Marilee was furious.

"How *could* you make up a vicious lie like that?" Marilee asked. "Do you think that just because I won some money that I don't have any feelings?"

"But I—"

"You followed me into the woods to tell me that? Of all the sick tricks! I came down out of the tree to be nice to you, and this is what I get in return? My mother is dead. D-E-A-D. Dead. Get it?"

The woman didn't flinch. "Your father's name is Allan," she said. "He—"

"You read that in the newspaper," Adam interrupted, trying to help. "Look, we'll help you find your way out of here, and help you get to wherever you live. Ma'am?"

The woman didn't appear to have heard what Adam was saying. She was staring at Marilee as she started talking again. "Your father and I were having . . . problems. He decided to do something about it. He kidnapped you."

Marilee turned to Adam, and the pain on her face was palpable. "This hurts too much, Adam," she said, barely able to get the words out. "Let's go."

"You don't believe me," the woman surmised sadly. "Can't you see it? I look at you, it's like looking in a mirror."

Marilee looked deep into her soul, and took pity on the woman. She must have such a hard life. "Look, no offense, ma'am, but I look nothing like you."

"The same hair, the eyes, and the cheekbones, see?" The woman put her hand to her own cheek.

"Come on, Marilee," Adam said. "She's a little confused. Let's just help her get to—"

"I can prove it," the woman said. She cocked her head at Marilee's right arm, hidden under the material of her designer jacket. "You were born with a heart-shaped birthmark there, on the inside of your forearm."

Marilee's jaw dropped. That information hadn't been published in any of the articles about her. The woman pushed the sleeve of Marilee's jacket up her arm and turned it over.

And there it was.

"But that doesn't prove anything," Adam insisted. "You could have seen Marilee somewhere when she had on short sleeves."

Marilee nodded agreement.

The woman came closer. Her right arm was shaking. She pushed up her own right sleeve.

There was a heart-shaped birthmark.

Exactly like Marilee's.

Chapter

12

"It's true," Marilee's father said.

Marilee backed up to a chair and sat down heavily, thinking there was no way her legs could support her weight.

She had gone right back to the hotel to talk with her father. The woman in the woods had to be lying. Or there had to be some reasonable explanation. Surely her father would explain it all as soon as she told him about it.

Only he hadn't.

Instead he'd just said, "It's true."

Mr. Ellis sat motionless on the plush couch, his face buried in his hands.

"All these years you've been *lying* to me?"

Marilee whispered, hurting so deeply she could barely speak. "Why?"

"To protect you."

"From *what?*"

"I hadn't been in San Diego six months when I met your mama," her father began. "I was working for a lawn service. One of the clients was a wealthy family by the name of Hermitage. They had a daughter, a real rebel named Melody, kind of a hippie girl, home for the summer after her freshman year of college. She was so beautiful. Untouchable by the likes of me, I figured.

"But one day I'm planting some flowers and she comes over, so we start talking. I was embarrassed to say I was from some Louisiana hick town called Carter, so I told her I was from Dallas, Texas—she thought that was exotic. I don't know where I got the nerve to ask her out, but I did. She said yes. Her parents, who already had big problems with her, were furious. But it didn't matter. We fell in love."

He looked at Marilee, to gauge how she was taking his story. Her face was unreadable.

"At the end of the summer," he went on, "Melody broke it to her parents: we were getting married, and if they tried to interfere we'd run away together and they'd never see her again. They didn't interfere, but they didn't come to the wedding, either. We got married at City Hall, in front of some friends and Grammy."

"Grammy," Marilee whispered. "Does Grammy know about—"

"I'll get to that," her father said. "The thing you need to know is, we were happy, Marilee. And we truly loved each other. And then . . ."

"What?"

He hesitated. "Your mama always did like a cocktail. Socially, you know. Then she started drinking alone, missing class and the like. They kicked her out of college. But she said that was fine because she had a little trust fund and what she really wanted was a baby. Right away. She swore she'd stop drinking to have it. And she did."

Me, Marilee thought, her head spinning. *I'm the baby.*

"You," her father said, confirming her thoughts. "But right after you were born, she started up again."

"You should have gotten help for her, then," Marilee told her father. "You were her *husband*. We were a *family*."

"I tried, Marilee, I swear I did. It didn't work. I went to her parents and they wouldn't talk to me. She went to treatment, to AA, but then I'd find bottles hidden all over the house. Alcoholism is a disease, honey."

Marilee swallowed, more stark photos of the truth flashing through her brain. She wished that Karly was with her. Or Adam.

But even if they had been, what she was hearing wouldn't hurt any less.

"Go on," Marilee told her father, gulping hard.

Mr. Ellis rubbed his hands over his tired eyes. "One day I came home from work and I found you on the kitchen floor, crying and hungry. The stove was on. Your mother was passed out from drinking. That was when I knew. I couldn't leave you with her anymore. It was too dangerous."

Mr. Ellis looked down, unable to look at his daughter.

"That's it, Daddy? That's your excuse?" Marilee felt like she should be crying. But somehow, the tears would not come.

"Don't you see, sweetie? The house could have burned down. You could have died! So I picked you up, got in the car, and came back to Carter. Lied and told Grammy that Melody had died in a car wreck."

"And if my mother or her parents had ever tried to find us, they would have looked in Dallas, because that's where you said you were from," Marilee reasoned aloud.

Her father nodded. "Marilee, sweetie, once you hit the Lotto and it was all over the news, I figured it was only a matter of time until she heard about you. I hoped she'd be clean and sober. With a new life and a family of her own."

So that she wouldn't want me anymore, Marilee thought dully. *So my own mother wouldn't want me.*

"I love you, Marilee," her father said in a shaky voice. "More than my life."

Marilee got up and walked around the suite. Suddenly all the nice things in it didn't seem so nice anymore. They were just things. They couldn't give her back her past. Or give her back a life with the truth.

"*Love?*" Marilee repeated dully. "That's not love. How do I know that you're telling me the truth now? You always told me my mother was this angel. I was so afraid I could never live up to how perfect she was—"

"Because I didn't want you to think badly of her—"

Marilee looked at her father directly "I believed you, Daddy. Do you know how much that hurts?"

Her father nodded, his eyes filled with tears.

As mad and hurt and confused as she was, her heart went out to him. Because she knew with all her heart that her father really did love her.

She went over to him and took his hand. "You were afraid to tell me the truth."

Her father sighed.

"That's it, isn't it?" Marilee went on, her voice small. "That's why you always act like you hate rich people so much? Because of how her parents rejected you? Because you're afraid it's because you didn't measure up to them? And it's why you gave up on your dreams, too. Because you're afraid to try. Because you're afraid you'd fail."

He gave her a watery smile. "I have one smart daughter."

"And what about Grammy?" Marilee asked. "Does she know all this?"

"Now she does," her father said. "After you won the Lotto, I told her. Are you ever gonna be able to forgive me, sweetie?"

Marilee got up. "I hope so. But the truth is . . . I don't know."

Joey was parked in front of the hotel when Marilee ran past him. He called to her, but she ignored him. So he got in the car and followed her—all the way to Adam's apartment above Overton Naturals.

Marilee knocked, and Adam's face appeared at the door. He'd been expecting her.

When they'd come out of the woods, they gave the woman who claimed to be Marilee's mother a ride to the inexpensive motel where she was staying. Marilee had handed the woman two hundred dollars. Then, Adam offered to be with Marilee when she talked with her father, but she said she had to do it alone, and that she'd come over to Adam's afterward.

Now, Adam took one look at her face, and without saying a word, came outside and took Marilee into his arms.

They held each other for a very long time.

They went and sat at the picnic table out behind the health food store, where she told him everything her father had told her.

"Unbelievable," he said, shaking his head. "I'm so sorry, Marilee. That you have to go through this."

She swallowed down the lump in her throat. She still had not cried. "How could he have lied to me? For all these years? How?"

Adam had no answer.

She shredded the tissue Adam had handed her between her fingers. "I hate him for this."

"You hate what he did, you mean."

"Well, how do you separate people from their actions? It's like I don't even know him. Like I never did."

Adam reached for her hand. "You can work this out with him, Marilee. It'll take time, but you can do it. You love him, Marilee. I know you do. He's your father."

"Don't tell me who I love, okay?" she retorted, her pent-up feelings spilling out of her. "The only one I love is you."

Her words hung in the air, suspended.

She couldn't take them back.

"I love you, Adam," she confessed. "I've loved you for a long time."

"Marilee—"

"But I was so afraid you didn't love me back."

"Marilee—"

"Adam, don't you see? I have more money than we could ever need. And I know Olivia is pretty, but she's such a terrible person. How could you—"

"Marilee, stop." He wrapped his hand around her wrist. "You think I love Olivia?" he asked, aghast.

Her eyes grew huge. "You don't?"

"I don't even *like* Olivia most of the time."

Marilee was stunned. "But you went to Logan's party with her."

"Olivia invited me because her family is friends with the Calhouns. She said there'd be a lot of Fairmonts at the party and I'd have a chance to get to know them so that I could start writing songs about them."

"But Livy called you her *boyfriend*. I *heard* her."

Adam got up, picked up a piece of newspaper that had blown into the backyard, and balled it up.

"After what just happened to you, Marilee, you should know that just because someone says something, doesn't make it true."

"Well, you didn't deny it."

"You never gave me the chance."

Marilee looked down, embarrassed. "I guess I didn't," she acknowledged.

A thought hit Marilee, and she bounced to her feet, incredibly excited. "Adam, do you have any idea how much I hate Overton? And everyone in it? You and I, we don't have to stay here. We can run away together, to—to New York. No one will find us there. No one will look there."

"Marilee—"

"You'll be able to record your songs in the best studios with the best musicians," Marilee went on, planning aloud. "It'll be so fantastic. We can leave all of this behind us and never look back. Oh, Adam, I love you so much!"

She flung her arms around him, hugging him.

And then she realized something.

He wasn't hugging her back.

She pulled away from him. She saw it in his eyes. He didn't love her. He was just too nice to say it.

Marilee's hand flew to her mouth. But there was no way to take the words back.

"Oh, no," she whispered.

It was, in some ways, even worse than what had happened with her father.

Because Adam had always *really* told her the truth.

"You don't understand, Marilee—"

"Yes. I do."

She started to leave, but he caught her hand.

"No, you don't. Going to New York won't solve anything. You'd be doing just what your father did. Running away."

She pulled her hand away. "There's a difference between leaving and running away," Marilee told him. "I'm leaving. Leaving a hateful place."

"You think everyone here is hateful?"

"Yes."

"That's only because you're judging them as much as you think they're judging you," Adam said.

"That's not true—"

"It isn't? What about Logan Calhoun, then? She wanted to be your friend."

"Logan? You mean Livy's dear friend Logan?" Marilee asked. "What could Logan possibly have to say to me?"

Adam shook his head sadly. "Marilee, Logan wants to be a photographer. She told me. She saw the photo you took of the Calhoun house after the ice storm. She thought it was awesome. Her aunt told her you had taken it. *That's* why she wanted to get to know you. That's why I gave her your code at the hotel."

Marilee stood there, mute.

"You never read the note that she sent to you, did you?" Adam asked.

Marilee shook her head no. There was no sense in lying to Adam. "But she's friends with Olivia—"

"Used to be," Adam said. "Logan had a chance to really get to know Livy, and now she can't stand her. Livy can't stand her anymore, either. And she's also not too fond of me. Especially after I told her that I had no interest in being her boyfriend. Ever."

Marilee's jaw dropped open.

"You've hardly been at school," Adam noted, "so how would you know the hot Overton gossip? What happened, Marilee? We used to be able to talk to each other about everything."

You got gorgeous, she thought. *I fell in love with you.*

But she didn't say that. She just said, "Things changed."

"Yeah, you got rich," Adam said. His voice expressed his disgust.

"No, that's not what I—"

"I suggest you take a good look in the mirror, Marilee. You're rich. Big deal. You haven't worked at your photography since you won the Lotto. You blew off a nice girl who wanted to be your friend. You totally dissed Ms. Pfeffer. All you're worried about is getting back at Livy and Bree. What a waste of time."

Silence.

More silence.

"Thank you for that analysis of my flawed character," Marilee finally managed, hurt by the words that she knew in her heart were true. "How lame of me to come to you for support when my life has fallen apart."

Adam shoved his hands into his pockets. "Okay, that was a little harsh maybe, but I only said it because I—"

"It doesn't matter," Marilee interrupted. "I'm leaving, Adam. Going home. Wherever that is."

"Marilee—"

She ignored him and kept walking toward the alley that led to the street. One part of her hoped that Adam would follow her, to be with her, to share her pain. Another part hoped that he would leave her alone with her pain, her past, and what was left of her pride.

He left her alone.

Which, by the time she got home, she decided was exactly the right thing for him to have done. Anything was better than having him see more of how the last twenty-four hours had shattered her heart.

When Marilee got back to the hotel suite, her father wasn't there.

Karly was. How she had known to come over, Marilee didn't know. All she knew was that it was wonderful.

She told her friend all about her conversation with her father.

And with Adam.

"He doesn't love me, Karly," Marilee declared.

"Adam didn't say that," Karly pointed out.

"No, he told me what a horrible, self-centered person I am, instead. And you know what? He's right."

"Uh-oh, pity party time," Karly sang out. "Do I need to make a tissue run?"

"Shut up," Marilee said, laughing through her tears. "I'm allowed to wallow. My dad lied to me for my whole life. My mom is . . . someone I don't even know, and don't know if I want to know. And Adam doesn't love me."

Karly plucked the last two tissues from the sterling silver box next to the bed and handed them to Marilee. "Grammy loves you. And for whatever it's worth, I love you."

Marilee blew her nose loudly. "Thanks. Do you think I changed after I got rich?"

Karly thought a moment. "Kinda."

"Kinda in a bad way?"

Karly hesitated. "Kinda . . . yeah," she admitted. "I mean, okay, you hated being poor. And I don't blame you. But how much money you have—or didn't used to have—isn't who you are."

"I can't decide if that's deep or icky," Marilee said, wiping her eyes.

"Me, either," Karly agreed. "Anyway, what do I know? If I got millions all of a sudden, I'd probably get totally obnoxious. I brought something to cheer you up."

"What?"

"It's in the bathroom. Hold on, it's a surprise."

Marilee blew her nose again, as the hurt welled up in her heart once more.

"Look up," Karly said.

And there was Karly, with Dog in her arms.

"Dog!" Marilee cried, taking the black-and-white cat from Karly's arms and burying her face in his fur. "Oh, Dog!"

"I smuggled him in under my rain poncho," Karly admitted. "Along with a little litter box and some food."

"You're the best, Karly," Marilee said, as Dog began to purr in her arms.

"That's what Dave says. But this guy at church, Mark, keeps calling me. He has two tickets to the Offspring concert."

"You are a hopeless flirt," Marilee said.

"It's one of my skills," Karly agreed. She sat next to her friend. "Listen, you'll work all this out, Marilee."

"Yeah," Marilee whispered.

The phone rang, and Marilee snatched it up. It was the concierge, saying that Karly's dad was waiting for her downstairs. The girls hugged goodbye, and Marilee promised she'd call Karly later.

Then she went back into her bedroom and sat on her luxurious bed with Dog still in her arms. He jumped away to explore the suite, and she was all alone.

Where am *I going?* she asked herself. A gigantic lump of loneliness filled her throat. *I don't belong anywhere. Or with anyone. Because who am I, really? And who do I want to be?*

Her eyes lit on the Loverock, which sat on her ornate marble nightstand. She picked it up. Immediately, a picture flew into her mind.

The ribbon-cutting ceremony downtown. The cool girl in the geeky glasses.

Callie.

"After you found the Loverock, you said your life changed, Callie," Marilee whispered as if Callie could actually hear her. "At first it all seemed so wonderful, you know? I thought being rich would change my life. But even Karly said I was nicer before. And being rich didn't make Adam love me. At least before I got the Loverock he was my best friend. But now—now, he doesn't even like me anymore. And my father . . . my father . . ."

The tears fell again. She was just so sad and lonely.

"Oh, Callie," she sobbed, "I wish I could go back. Is that how you felt, too? I'm so lonely now, and I'm so scared. I wish I could go back to how it was when I didn't know about my mother or any of it, even if it meant being poor again. I wish I could go back."

What was done may be undone.

Marilee was so startled she stopped crying.

Why had that thought sprung into her mind? And what did that mean? She looked down at the Loverock in her hands. The shimmery feeling was surging through her body, growing.

Suddenly Marilee knew. "Reverse the mirror image," she said. "I can reverse it. If I sleep with the Loverock under my pillow."

She dropped the rock. Because what she'd just said sounded truly crazy. But she wasn't crazy. Just temporarily stressed. That had to be it.

Except that she *knew* what she'd thought was true.

She picked up the Loverock. She could sleep with it under her pillow and go back to being poor.

But was that what she really wanted?

What I really want is to go back to not knowing the truth about my parents, she realized. *And I want Adam to love me. But no matter what I do, even if I go back to being poor, I can't reverse what I know. And I can't make Adam do what he doesn't—*

The Loverock slipped from her hands. It skidded across the newspaper her father had left on the carpet and landed in the corner, next to the box of her father's personal possessions.

Marilee bent to pick up the Loverock and noticed that the box was cracked open. She took the lid off. Inside, on the top was an old photo album. In the corner was engraved ALLAN & MELODY.

I never saw that before, Marilee thought. *I didn't even know it existed.*

She lifted it from the box and took it to the couch.

She opened it.

There was a photo of her parents, only a few years older than she was now, with their arms around each other.

They looked so happy, so in love.

Her mother looked just like Marilee.

The next photo was her skinny father, shirtless, striking a mock muscle pose. *My mother must have taken that,* Marilee thought. There was a photo of her parents on the beach with a whole bunch of their friends, laughing and clowning around. There were more: her parents' wedding portrait. Her parents kissing. Her mother pregnant with her, her father with his hands proudly spanning her belly.

And then her, newborn Marilee. In her mother's arms. With her father's arms around them both. Below that, in a curly, feminine scrawl, her mother had written a caption.

The happiest woman in the world bringing the most beautiful, precious baby that ever was, Marilee Elizabeth Ellis, home from the hospital, with her proud dad.

Marilee's eyes filled with tears again. Her mother *had* loved her. Her parents had loved each other.

She had been created from that love. The truth of it had been captured forever in those photographs.

Marilee closed the album and hugged it to her chest.

She knew that the rest of the story was entirely up to her—to decide just what kind of person the baby in those photos would grow up to be.

Chapter

13

TWENTY MILLION DOLLAR CINDERELLA PRINCESS USED TO WORK HERE! read the sign in the window of Hava Java.

Well, she doesn't work here anymore, Marilee thought as she walked through the open door. But she associated the place so closely with waitressing that she instantly felt guilty about not putting on an apron and rushing around to serve the customers.

Ignoring the sidelong glances of the customers who recognized her, Marilee made her way to the cash register, where her former boss, Mr. Wilson, was ringing up the checks for a small line of customers. Marilee waited patiently until he was done.

"Well, lookee who's here," Mr. Wilson said, beaming at Marilee. "Cinderella herself. Win the Lotto and throw away that Hava Java waitress apron. Is that how it goes?" He winked at her to show that he was just kidding.

"Something like that." Marilee nodded distractedly.

"So, can I get you some coffee? On the house? What brings Cinderella to this humble abode this afternoon?"

"Actually, Mr. Wilson, I need to talk to your nephew. Do you think you could give me his home phone number?"

"Matthew?" Mr. Wilson asked.

"No, Marley."

"Yeah, same kid. That's his Rastafarian name. I suppose if he discovers jazz he'll start calling himself the Duke. Whatever. He's a little flaky, but he's a good kid."

"So would you mind giving me his—?"

"I can do one better than that. He's here."

"He is? Now?" Marilee was unprepared for this. She'd hoped to do what she had to do by telephone.

"I'm letting him use the old oven in the back to experiment with a Jamaican jerk-chicken recipe. His mama's allergic to the spices in it. Hey, Lisa!" Mr. Wilson called to one of the waitresses on the floor. "Can you tell Matth—I mean Marley—that someone's here to see him?"

"Sure, Mr. Wilson."

Marilee waited nervously as Lisa disappeared into the kitchen. And then, without warning, Marley came sauntering out of the kitchen toward her, wearing what looked to be the same baggy jeans and Bob Marley T-shirt he'd been wearing when they met. His dreadlocks were tied back with a Jamaican bandanna.

Marley's eyes lit up. "Hey, what you know?" he said in a lilting Jamaican accent. "It's Lotto Maniac Girl!"

"Could I please speak with you?" Marilee asked. "Privately?"

"I'll keep an eye on your chicken, Marley," his uncle offered. "Don't worry. I won't let it burn."

"Yeah mon," Marley agreed, nodding. He headed for a free table in the corner and Marilee followed him.

She was nervous. Who knew what to expect from a white suburban American kid who talked and acted like he'd been raised in the shanty-towns of Jamaica?

"So, you be rich now, Lotto Maniac Girl," Marley said. "Congratulations."

"Is that all you have to say? Congratulations?"

"I'm happy for you, girl," Marley added. "I hope it brings you peace and joy. How's dat?"

"Look, Marley, could you please stop talking like—" Marilee stopped herself. She had no right to tell him how to talk. Then she leaned forward, and dropped her voice. "Marley, you know that I won with your ticket."

Marley nodded. "No problem, mon. I give it to you. Dat makes it *your* ticket."

"But you bought it," Marilee insisted. "Which means if you hadn't given it to me, you would have won the Lotto."

Marley tilted his head back. "You sorry you won?"

"I don't think you understand, Marley," Marilee explained. "The right thing for me to have done was to have contacted you right after I won. But I was afraid you'd claim it all belonged to you. I'm really sorry."

"Okay." Marley nodded. " 'Nuff respect, then. Thanks for tellin' me." He started to get up.

Marilee stopped him. "Where are you going?"

He pointed to the kitchen. "My chicken be cookin'."

Mr. Wilson was right. His nephew *was* a little flaky.

"Look, you still don't get it, do you? I want to split the money with you," Marilee declared.

"Dat so?" He sat back down, picked up a salt shaker, poured a little salt on the table, and balanced the shaker neatly on edge against some of the salt grains.

That's just how I feel, Marilee thought. *Balancing on the edge. Between one kind of life and another.*

"You know, funny t'ing," Marley mused. "Until I walked out de kitchen just now, I had no idea dat Lotto Maniac Girl was de winner."

"You're kidding. You don't read the newspaper?" Marilee asked incredulously. "Or watch the news?"

"Never," Marley said.

"Well, now you know," Marilee said. "The taxes were huge, because I took the money in a lump sum, but still your half comes to—"

"One million," Marley said.

"Oh no, it's much more than that."

Marley held up one finger, and kept it up until Marilee finally understood what he meant.

He'd take one million dollars. No more.

"But—" Marilee began.

"One million," Marley confirmed. "And I tell you now, girl, I'll do some good wi'd it." He leaned toward her. Suddenly his accent was gone. "Marilee, the richest kid I know has been in drug rehab three times," he said earnestly. "I don't think lots of money is the way to go."

Marilee opened her purse, took out a piece of paper, and wrote down her phone number and secret password at the hotel for him. "Call me. I can have my bank transfer the money to you tomorrow. Okay?"

"Yeah, mon," Marley said, fully Jamaican once more. They both got up and he smiled at her. "I put dat money to good use. Help de children of Jamaica. One love, one heart, mon. Take care, Lotto Maniac Girl. 'Nuff respect."

When she got back from Hava Java, her father was standing at the hotel suite window, his back to Marilee. He turned to her, looking as if he'd aged ten years since the day before.

The day everything had changed.

She thought back on her day. She had been awake since dawn and left the suite before her father woke up. She didn't go to school. Instead, she walked for miles, all the way out to the Calhoun estate, then to the mobile home with the homemade animal shelter behind it.

The place that used to be home.

She sat in the Big Room with all her stray animals, except Dog, around her and tried to figure out what she wanted to do with her life.

It was funny that she hadn't cleaned out the trailer yet. Or found other homes for her animals. It was almost as if she was holding on to something, not sure what that something was.

You have to believe in yourself, Marilee.

She sat there for a long, long time.

Then she took out some paper and a pen and wrote three important, heartfelt letters. To Ms. Pfeffer, to apologize for abusing the gift of her friendship and mentorship. To Logan Calhoun, to apologize for icing her out instead of giving her a chance to become a friend.

And to her mother.
That was the hardest letter of all.

Dear Mother,
Dad told me the truth about what happened.
And now here's my truth. I don't know how I
feel. Part of me feels so hurt. That Dad lied to me
for my whole life. And that you didn't care
enough about me to find me a long time ago. I
guess the only place we can start is at the begin-
ning. But our beginning is right now. What hap-
pened between you and Dad has to remain
between the two of you. Because there's no way
for me to figure it out. Blaming and judging just
seems like a waste of time. And we've already lost
so much time, Mom. I'll help you any way I can.
And maybe you can help me, too. I always
dreamed about having a mom. I just never
thought it would really happen. I would like to
get to know you, if you would like to know me.
That's a good place to start.

Marilee

She spent the entire day out by the old
trailer, just playing with the animals and thinking. She had called her father on her cell phone
to tell him where she was. All he did was ask
that Joey Souffet confirm her whereabouts and
call him.

After calling her dad, Joey left her alone.

Finally in the midafternoon Marilee gave each of the animals a special hug, and then left.

To face the rest of her life.

Now she stood, looking at her father, filled with a jumble of emotions.

"You're back," he said softly, stating the obvious.

Marilee sat in a plush living room armchair. "We have to talk, Daddy."

"Right." He sat on the couch. "I talked to Grammy again and she told me to tell you how much she loves you. She said you just pick up the phone at any time and say, 'Grammy' and she'll be here for you the next instant."

Marilee smiled.

"I should have told you a long time ago, but . . . all I can say is, I'm sorry, Marilee," her father said after a long pause. "I haven't been the best father, I know that. But I've loved you with all my heart, from the day you were born. And no matter what you do, even if you decide you hate me, I'll love you with all my heart until the day I die."

Her father's eyes filled, and so did Marilee's heart. She ran across the room, flung her arms around him, and held him close.

He was still Daddy. And she still loved him.

And she told him that.

"Daddy," Marilee said, when they finally broke apart, "I have something else to tell you."

"Anything, honey."

"I found the person who gave me our winning ticket."

Mr. Ellis's eyes grew wide. "You did?"

"I offered him half the money."

A flicker of shock crossed Mr. Ellis's face. But then his better self took over.

"You did the right thing, sweetie," he said.

"All he would take is a million dollars."

"Why?" Her father looked bewildered.

"Marley is, uh, unique." Dog rubbed against her legs, and she bent down to stroke his fur. "I should have gone to him a long time ago, but I didn't. It was wrong."

"Don't be so hard on yourself—"

"That's just it, Dad. I think maybe I need to be a little harder on myself. No more lies, no more excuses. No blaming other people for the bad qualities I have in myself. That's not me. I mean, that's not the person I want to try to be. So I have to ask you, Daddy. What kind of person do you want to be?"

He looked at her with pride. "One who's a good example for a wonderful daughter like you." He hugged her close. "So, where does that leave us, Marilee?"

"I wrote to my mother. It still sounds so strange to say that. I want to see her this weekend. After that, I don't know. A lot will be up to her. And her parents, my grandparents. They could never be Grammy, but—"

Mr. Ellis stood and walked back over to the window. He picked something up from the ledge.

It was the photo album that Marilee had found, of Mr. and Mrs. Ellis and Marilee when she was a baby.

"You found this, huh?"

"Uh-huh."

"How did you get so smart, Marilee?" he asked, his voice husky with pride.

"Grammy," she replied truthfully.

Her father nodded.

"And you, Daddy. A lot of it is you."

"I'll be in the Big Room," she'd told Adam over the phone. "If you're free, I'd really like to talk to you."

Now, as she sat in the fading light of day in one of the plastic chairs that still sat outside the trailer, she watched him walk toward her.

So handsome. So familiar. So loved.

"Hi." He had his guitar with him.

"Hi."

"I'm glad you called me," he said. He put his guitar down and looked at the trailer. "Does living here seem real to you anymore?"

"Yeah," Marilee said. "I never, ever want to forget it. Especially this."

She clapped her hands three times and gave a special whistle, and from the other side of the trailer came two dogs and four cats on a dead run. They ran right to Marilee's feet, where they barked and meowed happily.

"So much love," Marilee said. "They don't care if I'm rich or poor. All they care about is that I care about them."

Adam dropped to his knees to wrestle with the dogs.

"There's more I don't want to forget," Marilee said.

Adam rolled one of the dogs over onto his back and tickled his stomach. "Like what?"

"Like loving someone doesn't mean you won't make mistakes." She looked around at the vast, lush green of the land. "Like that the Big Room really is the most beautiful room anywhere."

"Funny," Adam said softly, rising to his feet and taking in the view, "that's exactly what I always thought."

Marilee looked over her shoulder at the trailer. "The girl who lived here isn't me anymore, Adam. But neither is Cinderella. The only me there is, is . . . well, me."

He nodded, waiting for her to say more.

But it's just so hard to say, she thought. *And I still love him so much.*

"You were right," she whispered. "So much of what you said was—"

"Marilee," Adam interrupted her, "I could kick myself for yelling at you like I did, especially when you were hurting so much—"

"But it was true." Marilee gulped hard. "And what I said is true, too. How I feel about you. And I'm not sorry I told you, even though I know you don't love me—"

"Marilee—"

"I have to say it all before I lose my nerve," Marilee rushed on. "I mean, what good is so much money if I don't do some good with it? I want to build a rec center back in Carter. For kids. With a pool and a gym and rooms for art and music lessons. And photography. A darkroom, too, with good equipment. And I want to build an animal shelter where none of the animals waiting for homes have to be put to sleep. Where kids can volunteer. Animals don't care about money. All they care about is love."

"Marilee—" Adam began.

"There's more, Adam. I'm moving back to Carter after the school year."

Adam was shocked. "You're *what?*"

"Adam, I don't like Overton. I've always loved Carter. Grammy's there. And Karly. And a lot of kids who could use some help, and—"

"Oh, Marilee!"

The next thing she knew Adam was on his feet, and he'd lifted her out of her chair and into his arms.

"What?" she asked, startled.

"There's only one way to get a word into this monologue, Marilee Elizabeth Ellis," Adam said.

And then he gently pulled her to him and kissed her. "Do you have any idea how much I love you, Marilee?" he asked.

Her jaw dropped open. "You said—"

"No. I didn't say. *You* said."

"You *love* me?" she asked him, incredulous.

Adam laughed. "I've loved you forever, you dope! I've never loved anyone *but* you, Marilee. The real you. And I—well, I guess I just don't have any experience with how to deal with these things, but—"

"There's only one way to get a word into this monologue, Adam Benjamin Eagleton." She grabbed him and kissed him back with all the love in her heart.

When they pulled apart, he was smiling at her. She smiled back. She could be brave and honest.

Right now.

She opened her mouth. Just as he opened his.

"Would you go to the fall formal with me?" they both asked at the exact same time.

And then dissolved into gales of laughter. The cats and the dogs didn't really understand what was so funny, but they could feel the love between Adam and Marilee, and they happily scampered around, caught up in the feeling.

"I'd be honored," Adam told her.

"Mutual," Marilee said, grinning.

"What about the Y.A.A. project?" Adam asked her.

"If you write music for my entry, I'm in," Marilee said. "And if you're not in, I'm still in."

"That's how it's going to be, huh?"

"Yup," Marilee told him.

"You're quite a girl, Marilee. And I'm definitely in."

Then they kissed again, and it was the kind of kiss Marilee had only read about in romantic novels or imagined in her dreams. The perfect kiss from the perfect boy, in the most perfect room in the world.

Epilogue

From: Dr. Louise Warner, Chair, Substance Z project
To: Substance Z Recovery/Field Test Team
Re: Sub Z Effect on Subject Two (Marilee Ellis); Priorities
for the Future

Subject Two's transformation from poor girl to
Lotto winner has been positively attributed to
the Mirror Image Effect resulting from her contact with Sub Z in her so-called Loverock.

Subject Two has not reversed the MIE, as did Subject One. At this time we are reducing Subject Two's level of surveillance to Level Six; resources previously devoted to Subject Two are being diverted to our efforts to identify new subjects.

New computer models of the explosion of the Subbie satellite indicate that many more chunks than we had previously thought returned to earth in and around the New Orleans metropolitan area.

To that end, the Substance Z recovery team is redoubling its efforts to identify and then track any and all people, especially teen girls, who may have come into possession of chunks of activated Substance Z.

Finding and tracking these people is of the highest possible priority.

READ THIS MEMO CAREFULLY. THEN SHRED IT.

About the Authors

CHERIE BENNETT and JEFF GOTTESFELD have written or co-written many well-loved series for teens, including *Teen Angels*, *Sunset Island*, *Wild Hearts*, and now *Mirror Image*. Cherie also writes hardcover fiction, including the award-winning *Life in the Fat Lane* and *Zink*. She is also one of America's finest young playwrights (*Anne Frank & Me*, *Searching for David's Heart*), a two-time New Visions/New Voices playwriting winner at the Kennedy Center. Her Copley News Service teen advice column, *Hey Cherie!*, is syndicated nationally. Cherie and Jeff celebrate their tenth anniversary next year; they live in Los Angeles and Nashville. Contact them at P.O. Box 150326, Nashville, TN 37215; or at authorchik@aol.com.

Todd Strasser's

Here Comes Heavenly

Look for a new title every other month starting in
October 1999

Here Comes Heavenly

She just appeared out of nowhere. Spiky purple hair, tons of
earrings and rings. Hoops through her eyebrow and nostril,
and tattoos on both arms. She said her name was Heavenly
Litebody. Our Nanny. Nanny???

Dance Magic

Heavenly is cool and punk. She sure isn't the nanny our
parents wanted for my baby brother, Tyler. And what's with
all these ladybugs?

Pastabilities

Heavenly Litebody goes to Italy with the family and causes all
kinds of merriment! But...is the land of amore ready for her?

Spell Danger

Kit has to find a way to keep Heavenly Litebody, the Rand's
magical, mysterious nanny from leaving the family
forever.

 Available from Archway Paperbacks
Published by Pocket Books

2307

Jeff Gottesfeld and Cherie Bennett's

MIRROR IMAGE

When does a dream become a nightmare?
Find out in MIRROR IMAGE as a teenage girl
finds a glittering meteorite, places it under her pillow,
and awakens to discover that her greatest wish
has come true...

STRANGER IN THE MIRROR

Is gorgeous as great as it looks?

RICH GIRL IN THE MIRROR

Watch out what you wish for...

STAR IN THE MIRROR

Sometimes it's fun to play the part
of someone you're not
...until real life takes center stage.

FLIRT IN THE MIRROR

... From tongue-tied girl to the ultimate flirt queen.

From Archway Paperbacks

Published by Pocket Books

In time of tragedy, a love that would not die...

Hindenburg, 1937
By Cameron Dokey

San Francisco Earthquake, 1906
By Kathleen Duey

Chicago Fire, 1871
By Elizabeth Massie

Washington Avalanche, 1910
By Cameron Dokey

---

sweeping stories of star-crossed romance

Starting in July 1999

From Archway Paperbacks
Published by Pocket Books

2103